THE ART OF MISSING LINK ™

THE ART OF

MISSING LINK

™

Written by Ramin Zahed

Foreword by Stephen Fry

Introduction by Chris Butler

INSIGHT EDITIONS

San Rafael, California

CONTENTS

FOREWORD

BY STEPHEN FRY

The jobbing actor, if they are lucky, can expect many surprises in their journey through life and work. Some are unpleasant ("Regretfully we thought you were too old/fat/English/eccentric/obvious for this role"), some delightful ("The locations for the shoot will be Sardinia, Seville, Amsterdam, Rome, and Antigua"), and some baffling ("Your legs will be replaced by digital wheels and, with the use of green screen, you will be given antennae and six flappable ears") . . . but it would be a churl and an ingrate who complained at the opportunity and variety the profession offers.

Over the last decade or so, actors have been called upon to lend their voices to more and more animated features as the medium has continued to expand and grow. It may be that, like me, you deplore the tendency to demystify the techniques of film production, so I won't go into too much detail about process, other than to restate what any viewer of DVD and streaming extras and publicity B-roll will already know. No matter how many characters share a given scene, you will record your voice alone. It will all be done months, if not years, before there exists any visual element for you to respond to beyond drawings and enthusiastic verbal descriptions. Voice actors find themselves alone in glass booths for days on end barking, whispering, growling, and shouting "Whoooooaaaaaahhh!" as they fall from great heights. (The characters I play always seem to fall from great heights, and I am called upon to "whoooooaaaaaahhh" a lot. I may hold a world record.) The consequence of this manner of working is that by the time the picture is ready for its release eighteen months to two years later, you will have forgotten all about it. So when your agent calls you up to tell you you've been invited to the premiere, you find yourself saying:

"Well, that's very kind, I'm sure. Why would they want me there?"

"You play Anstruther the Turtle."

"I do?"

And a dim memory of having to chew lettuce and tick off the hero (before falling from a cliff) returns to you.

"Oh yes. But I played him as a tortoise, not a turtle. Well, well. Wonder how it's all turned out."

In the case of *Missing Link*, I suffered from no such failures of recall. Indeed I spent the year and a half following my contribution feverishly wondering when the finished movie would have its first screening.

The difference is LAIKA. You may be aware of their work and how it has always stood out from the crowd—*Coraline*, *ParaNorman*, *The Boxtrolls*, *Kubo and the Two Strings*. That glorious stop-motion animation. The characterization. The storytelling. The exquisite designs of everything from the leaves on background trees to the buttons on waistcoats. Always a look and a feel that is above the common run. Not archly and pointlessly artsy, but richly and purposefully fine. Classy but approachable.

One difference was LAIKA, but the other was writer-director Chris Butler. Every beat of story and every frame of animation was under his eye, and the visits I made to the sound studio to record were like visits to the combined art gallery, design studio, and museum of late-Victorian costume, transport, and imperial manners that lived inside his brain. Each time the work became richer, fuller, funnier, and more rewarding as Chris enlivened me with his vision of the world he was creating.

You will see something of Michael Todd's *Around the World in 80 Days*, of course, and something of *The Lost World* and other films of that steampunk adventure genre (*Twenty Thousand Leagues Under the Sea*, *Journey to the Center of the Earth*, etc.), but you will find originality and a gentle but firm underpinning of twenty-first-century satire, too. Without a trace of schmaltz or sanctimonious piety, *Missing Link* tells a tale of man's exploitation of nature, indigenous peoples, and species that is worth attending to. And, like the best grand, adventurous epics, it manages to present an enchantingly intimate story of friendship as well. The missing link, it turns out, is understanding.

Ars est celare artem the old Latin tag has it: Art conceals its artistry. The following lickably lavish and lovely pages offer a glimpse of the astounding attention to detail, the thousands and thousands of hours, the slow, grueling, and painstaking concentration, and, yes, the ferocious and inspiring love that goes into the preparation, production, and completion of a LAIKA movie. Enjoy.

INTRODUCTION

BY CHRIS BUTLER

Art can do funny things to a nascent creative mind. A splash of acrylic on canvas, or the smudge of graphite on a toothy scrap of paper, perhaps the curve of an architectural cornice, or even the careful sweep of limbs across a floodlit stage . . . all have the ability to shape the hungry young imaginations of those who see them.

Film is, of course, an art form. And what is animation if not the perfectly cultivated coalescence of artificial expression in film? A fantastical illusion played out within a purely fabricated reality in which every trinket, tchotchke, doodad, and thingamabob is designed, engineered, and assembled. It is art on top of art on top of art. Art squared, if you like.

Film, and the sweet delights of animation, fed my own insatiable munchies of the mind. For decades I dined on a diet of dishes from Walt Disney, Steven Spielberg, George Lucas, and Ray Harryhausen. Now, I'm not one for hyperbole, but without a doubt, hands down, beyond question, the best movie ever made in the history of the universe is *Raiders of the Lost Ark*. I reveled in its pulpy mélange of whip-cracking action and swashbuckling derring-do, its deft dance between history and mythology, its larger-than-life characters running the gamut from drama to romance to comedy. When I saw it as a suggestible youth, it pretty much shook my percolating creativity into a big frothy mess of fantastical possibilities.

And when I wasn't discovering the cinematic delights of beating up Nazis in the name of archaeology, I was eagerly watching and reading the countless filmic and literary iterations of a different kind of hero. As he probed the darkest mysteries of the Victorian age, eccentric genius Sherlock Holmes had me equally thrilled and tantalized.

When it came time to develop my next movie at LAIKA, I dove eagerly into this well of influence. I wanted to create a character who was a little bit Indiana Jones, a little bit Sherlock Holmes, and a little bit of every other barrel-chested adventurer of yesteryear's ripping yarns. Passionate and idiosyncratic and scientifically minded and ready to surmount any obstacle in pursuit of his prize. And what better exploit for this dashing animated daredevil than the search for mythical creatures? Basically, I figured if I was going to throw all my childhood inspirations into a pot, the stew was going to be seasoned with cool Harryhausen-esque primitive beasts.

The yang to Sir Lionel's yin is the Missing Link himself. If Lionel is a nod to Holmes, then Link is his very hairy Watson. He's basically what you'd get if you crossed John Candy from *Planes, Trains and Automobiles* with Mighty Joe Young. Stop-motion has a rich history of soulful primates (with Kong being the granddaddy of them all), so it seemed the perfect medium with which to realize our hirsute hero.

The setting of the story is the Victorian age, a time of dynamic change in which an insular Old World experienced the shock of the new. It offered us a chance to explore a vibrant landscape at once familiar and extraordinary, while also providing a timely plight for our protagonists. The movie is a passionate cry for broadening horizons and breaking down walls. It's about opening doors, not closing them.

It's also a movie about names. What's *in* a name, to be specific. It's about how the names we give ourselves are far more important than those that are put upon us by others.

You'll find plenty of names in this book. A plethora of artists whose hard graft and creativity brought this project to life. In truth there are many names that didn't make it into these pages—names no less important to the production but too legion to fit. You'll see them all in the end credits of the movie, and you should know that every single one of them played an integral part. There's a crew photograph somewhere near the back of this book that reveals the veritable army of stalwart soldiers in the trenches of a production like this. I'd wager that every person in that picture, at some point in their childhood, saw a movie, or perhaps a piece of art in a book like this, and it lit within them that furious fuse of inspiration, and it made them think, *I want to do that*. And they did.

This book, this collection of art, is for everyone who is about to think, *I want to do that*.

1
LONDON

❧

"If I'm ever to be taken seriously by the adventuring community, I must provide proof."
—Sir Lionel Frost

Our hero makes his home in Victorian-era London. Quickly abandoned by his latest valet, Sir Lionel is left alone with nothing but thirst for his next adventure—an adventure he desperately hopes will gain him the acceptance of his peers.

❦

FIG. 1

"I wanted London to look busy, noisy, and bustling. Its inhabitants are the most removed from nature that we have in the story, and though they are from varied walks of life, I felt they should generally look pretty pleased with themselves as their city heads into the modern age."

——— WARWICK JOHNSON CADWELL
CHARACTER DESIGN AND CONCEPT ILLUSTRATION

FIG. 4

FIG. 5

PAGES 12–13: August Hall

FIG. 1: Warwick Johnson Cadwell

FIG. 2: Ross Stewart

FIG. 3: Santiago Montiel

FIG. 4: Ross Stewart

FIG. 5: August Hall

FIG. 2

FIG. 3

INTRODUCING

SIR LIONEL FROST

Sir Lionel Frost is a fearless, charismatic adventurer and one of the main protagonists of *Missing Link*. Sir Lionel is voiced by Hugh Jackman, whom director Chris Butler says he was thinking about while doing early character drawings. "We usually spend a good amount of time trying to find the actor or actress who fits the character best, but for this movie, I wanted Hugh, and I wasn't going to accept anyone else!" With Jackman in mind, Sir Lionel's design evolved, resulting in a character who is swashbuckling but stately, a broad-shouldered gentleman with a chiseled jaw. Described as a cross between Indiana Jones, Sherlock Holmes, and James Bond, Sir Lionel Frost is a privileged aristocrat who is always dressed in the latest fashions of the era. He can be self-centered and callous, and a bit of a Casanova, but he redeems himself through the course of the movie. As he travels the world to prove the existence of mythical creatures, he maintains an earnest appreciation for every new wonder he encounters.

FIG. 1

FIG. 2

FIG. 3

FIG. 1: Chris Butler

FIG. 2: Louis Thomas

FIG. 3: Warwick Johnson Cadwell

FIG. 4

FIG. 5

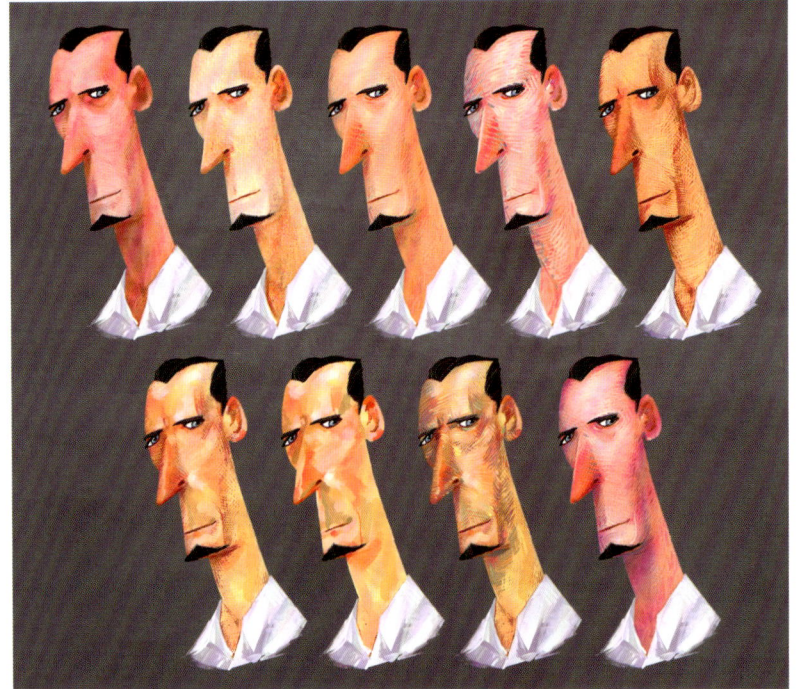

A key collaborator in the character design for *Missing Link* was illustrator Warwick Johnson Cadwell (the No. 1 Car Spotter and Helena Crash book series), who is known for his playfully idiosyncratic drawings. "When he draws a period illustration, it is so full of authentic details, you can almost smell it," explains Butler, who has been a fan of Johnson Cadwell's work for years. "When I started the project, I had a pretty good idea of what I wanted the characters to look like, but I needed something extra to bring them all to life. I turned to Warwick, who ended up sketching the entire world of this movie . . . animals, props, people in the street . . . illustrations both beautifully observed and wildly asymmetrical. I took my drawings and put them right through a Warwick filter—and that became the look of our movie."

FIGS. 4 & 5: Chris Butler and Trevor Dalmer

FIGS. 6, 7 & 8: Juliaon Roels

FIG. 6   FIG. 7   FIG. 8

FIG. 1

FIG. 2

FIGS. 1 & 2: Chris Butler

FIG. 3: Max Narciso

MORE
BUSTER CRABBE
THAN CAPTAIN
AMERICA.

FIG. 3

FIG. 1

FIG. 2

FIG. 3

"Early in the development process, I adapted a sketch by Warwick [Johnson Cadwell], incorporating all the ideas I wanted to explore: symmetry, dense contrasting patterns, clutter vs. negative space . . . the whole bag of tricks. Trevor Dalmer painted it, and I said, 'This is the movie!' This became our eureka moment."

—— CHRIS BUTLER
WRITER-DIRECTOR

FIG. 1: Warwick Johnson Cadwell
FIG. 2: Chris Butler
FIG. 3: Chris Butler and Trevor Dalmer
FIG. 4: Nelson Lowry

"The characters that Chris Butler created were broadly stylized. The style guide was created to help communicate fundamental rules of simplification and patterning for the world they would inhabit."

——————— *NELSON LOWRY*
PRODUCTION DESIGNER

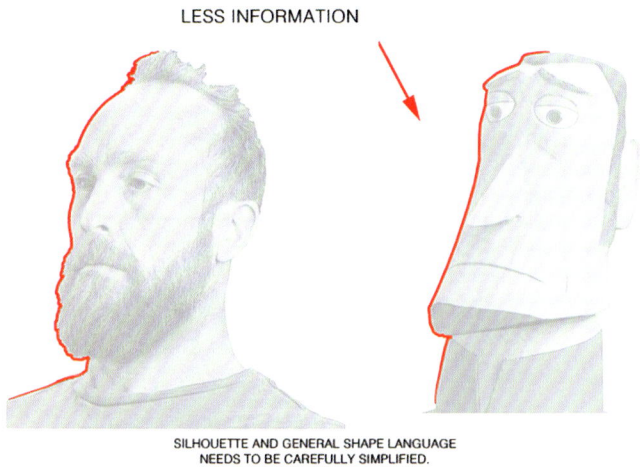

LESS INFORMATION

NOTICE HOW THE CHARACTERS MORE READILY BREAK DOWN INTO SIMPLER SHAPES

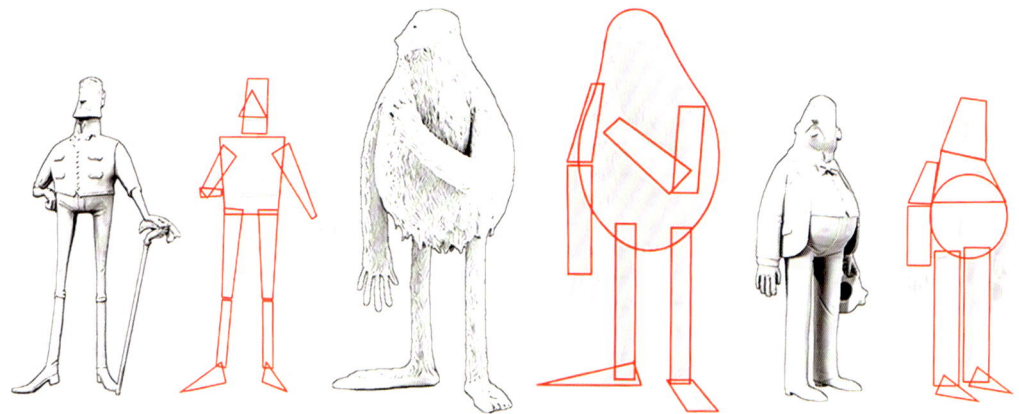

SILHOUETTE AND GENERAL SHAPE LANGUAGE
NEEDS TO BE CAREFULLY SIMPLIFIED.

COLOR MIXING WITH PATTERN IS PREFERED
WHENEVER POSSIBLE

STRONG PATTERNING RUNS THROUGH ALL ASPECTS
OF THE SHOW (VISIT SHOTGUN FOR DETAILS)

THERE ARE MANY PATTERNS
AVAILABLE ON SHOTGUN!

EVEN SMALL DETAILS FOLLOW THESE RULES...

REAL   ML
TORN PAPER

REAL   ML
ROCK

FIG. 4

FIG. 1

SIR LIONEL'S LIVING QUARTERS

Butler's fascination with Victorian England expresses itself in his depiction of our hero's cluttered office, which is the takeoff point of all his adventures. Sir Lionel is an obsessive and flawed character, traits his quarters reflect. In the script, his flat is described as "equal parts bachelor pad, dime museum, and mad scientist's laboratory."

"The room is thematically divided to reflect Sir Lionel's inner conflict," says art director Rob DeSue. "On one side you have this freewheeling monster-chaser side, while the other part you have this dominant wall of portraits, representing order and the establishment, as well as disapproving relatives. So you get this indication that when Lionel is in his study, he lives between these two worlds."

Production designer Nelson Lowry says the objects found in Lionel's home are directly informed by what Butler wanted to express about the hero. "We start with an assumption about the character based on what the director tells us," he elaborates. "We know that he's a cryptozoologist in turn-of-the-century London, and that he is kind of a rogue. We look for things that fit and help reinforce that character. Ultimately, everything is in that room for a reason, and nothing is completely arbitrary."

"With the portraits of Sir Lionel's ancestors, I was focused on trying to make them feel like old, authentic oil paintings that have been put through our film's simplification and stylization process. The forebears' judgmental expressions needed to have a clear readability for quick shots."

—— *TREVOR DALMER*
CONCEPT ARTIST

FIG. 2

FIG. 3

FIG. 1: Warwick Johnson Cadwell

FIG. 2: Louis Thomas

FIG. 3: Trevor Dalmer

FOLLOWING PAGES: Juliaon Roels and Trevor Dalmer

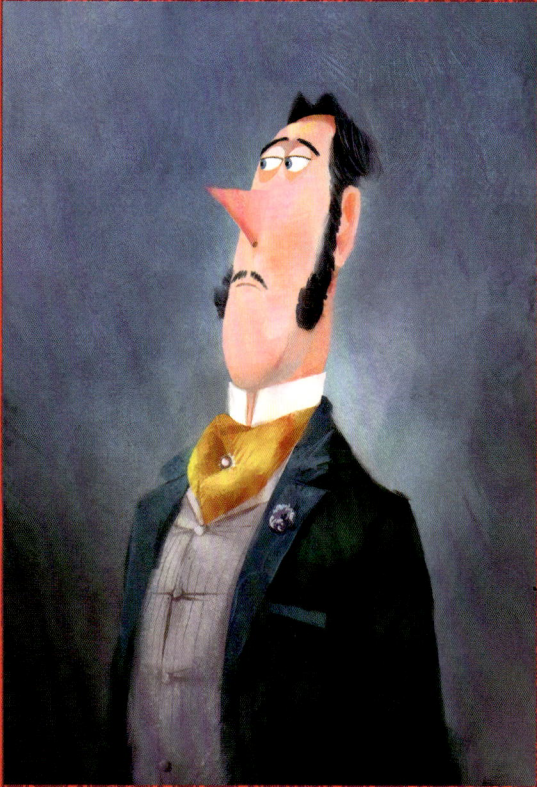

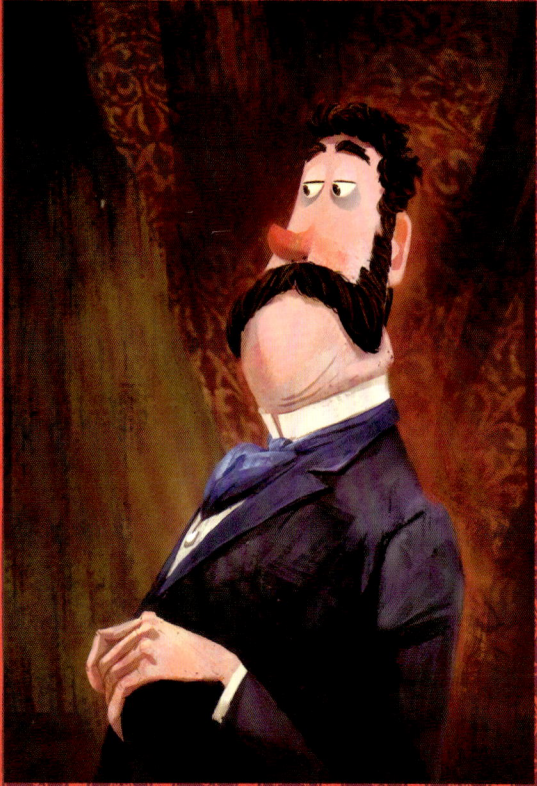

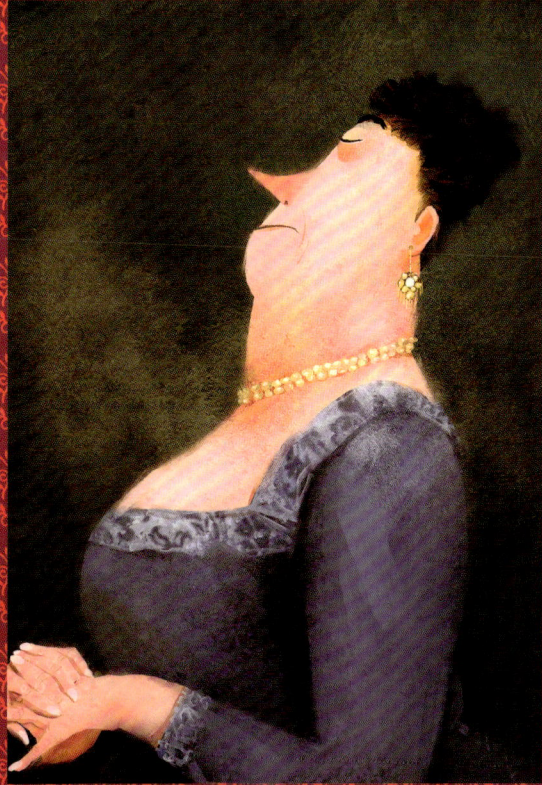

FIG. 1

"It was so much fun to research and curate this historic tableau of tools and strange artifacts unique to the Victorian era, and adapt them to our movie. If you have a quick eye, you'll spot some special Easter eggs nestled in."

—— PHIL BROTHERTON
ASSISTANT ART DIRECTOR

"Some of the items cluttering Sir Lionel's study are little in-jokes that we couldn't resist. Book titles that refer to the movie's literary influences (Arthur Conan Doyle's The Lost World *and* Sherlock Holmes*) and artifacts from previous movies."*

—— CHRIS BUTLER
WRITER-DIRECTOR

FIG. 2

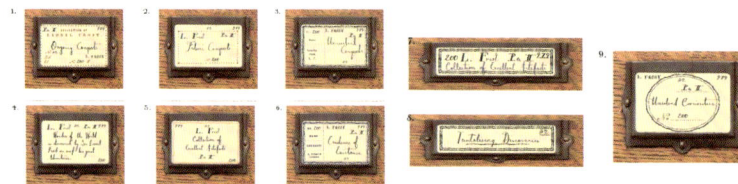

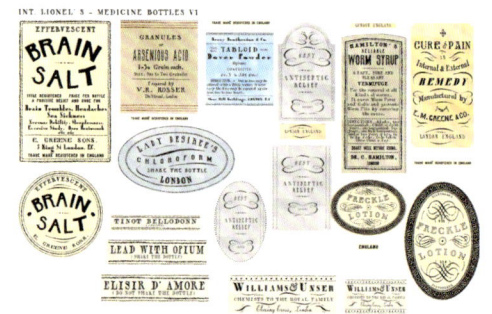

FIG. 3

FIG. 4

FIG. 5

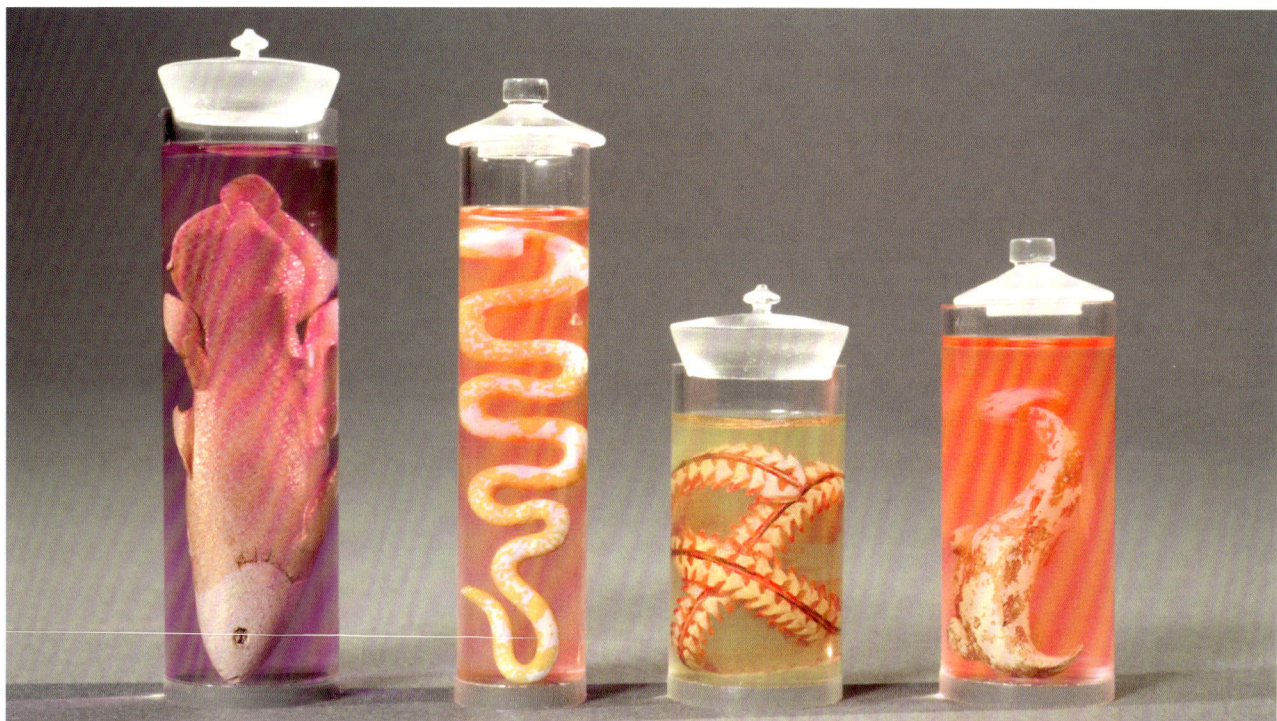

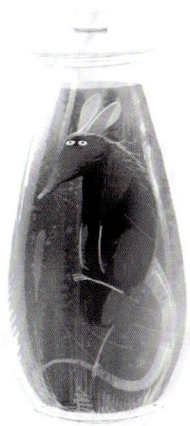

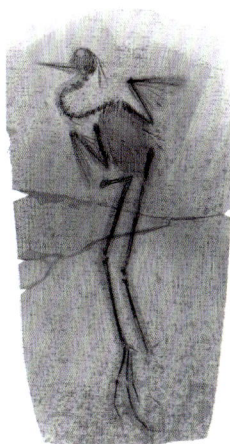

FIG. 1: Juliaon Roels and Desiree Ong

FIG. 2: Juliaon Roels and Phil Brotherton

FIG. 3: Jane Brodie

FIG. 4: Warwick Johnson Cadwell

FIG. 5: Juliaon Roels

THE OPTIMATES CLUB

The elite gentleman's club where Sir Lionel Frost confronts his adversary Lord Piggot-Dunceby stands in deep contrast to the colorful world depicted in the rest of the movie. In a nod to the famous Explorers Club of the Victorian age, the script describes the headquarters as "all black wood, white marble" and "as chilly as a mausoleum." Indeed, the setting for the stuffy gentlemen-only club was initially going to be created in black and white.

As Rob DeSue explains, "Our goal was to make the most colorful film we had ever made, so we challenged ourselves not to use black in this sequence. Even the part of the film that was intentionally perceived as black and white was actually rich in color." Nelson Lowry developed original concepts for the Optimates Club interiors, in which color was applied carefully throughout even the darkest areas of the hall. "The club members' black suits were actually a dull, dark violet," Lowry says, "and behind the black-and-white wood grain on the walls was a base coat of pale yellow, pink, and green." In the end, the nearly black-and-white hues of the club helped highlight the lords' conservative stubbornness and maintain a connection to the otherwise colorful nature of the film. "We learned how to make even dull and drab places seem alive, have a history, and exude a clear vibrancy. But in the end, compared to the other colors in the world, this backdrop feels like black and white," says DeSue.

"It was an entertaining challenge to keep the shocked and defeated expressions of the Optimates' taxidermy when sculpting and covering them with texture. Materials for fur ranged from the carefully trimmed and styled faux fur on the bear to finely cut paper on the monkey."

— EMILY NEILSON
LOOK DEVELOPMENT ARTIST

"The taxidermied animals are morbid objects we used to show the cruelty of the club, so we chose to design rare and cute animals to help emphasize how far the club would go."

— JULIAON ROELS
CHARACTER DESIGN
AND CONCEPT ARTIST

THIS PAGE: Concept art by Juliaon Roels
FOLLOWING PAGES: Ken Pak and Nelson Lowry

INTRODUCING
LORD ——
PIGGOT-
DUNCEBY

✖

Sir Lionel's main adversary and foil is a reactionary explorer. While Lionel likes to travel the world because he finds it endlessly fascinating, Piggot-Dunceby only wants to conquer it. "His name truly says it all," explains Chris Butler. "He is both a bigot and a dunce."

Although Piggot-Dunceby and Lionel have different philosophies, they are essentially the same kind of character—"overprivileged British aristocrats," notes Butler. There were also many similarities in terms of design. "They both have very blocky, robust frames, almost barrel-chested," Butler points out. "In one of Warwick's early drawings, Piggot-Dunceby is depicted as an old military gent with an eye patch on, and he looked like an absolute arse. As pleasingly vile as he was, we eventually moved away from this concept, because the full beard was potentially problematic for the puppet's printed faces. I also pushed the character's features to be closer to Lionel. He was more chiseled, with a strong jawline and a sharper nose. He's like Lionel in twenty years' time if he made a lot of bad decisions."

FIGS. 1, 5 & 6: Juliaon Roels

FIGS. 2 & 4: Warwick Johnson Cadwell

FIG. 3: Chris Butler

FIG. 1

FIG. 2

FIG. 3

FIG. 4

FIG. 5

FIG. 6

FIG. 1

FIG. 2

FIG. 3

FIG. 1: Juliaon Roels
and Chase Nichol

FIG. 2: Warwick Johnson
Cadwell

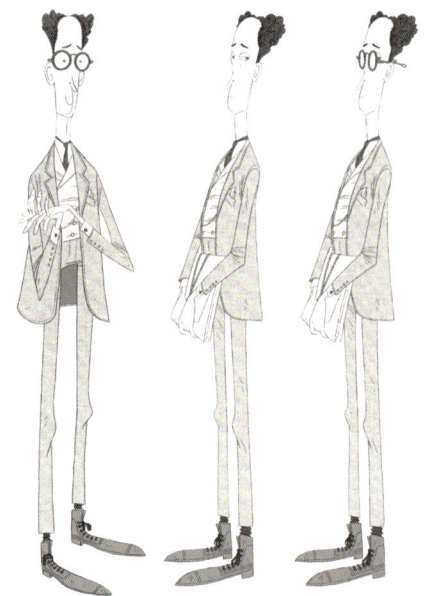

FIG. 3: Chris Butler

FIG. 4: Brian Ormiston

Business:

FIG. 4

cleaning glasses

bravo
Piggot

you did it
again Piggot

best telling
yet
Piggot

smoothing comb over.

your bloodiest
one so far
Piggot

winding pocket watch

adjusting bow tie

masterful

zzz...
mumble
mumble

Caressing rim of brandy glass

most ruthless
piggot,
top notch.

carving
a peach

drooling

The change over the group when Lionel says his word
is good, what is Piggots word worth... a shade of doubt
passes through the men, eyes now on Piggot. Piggot needs to
win back his
audience.

ONLY THE FINEST VICTORIAN THREADS

Costume designer Deborah Cook, who was nominated for a Costume Designers Guild Award in the Excellence in Fantasy Film category for her work on *Kubo and the Two Strings*, has worked on all of LAIKA's films to date. She and her team spent many months researching the details that would inspire the costumes of *Missing Link*. Each costume had to not only reflect the authentic fashions of the Victorian era but also speak volumes about the details of the key characters.

"One of our points of reference was Victorian-era artist William Morris's patterns and wallpapers," Cook points out. "We brought in some of that dense pattern-making and hard silhouette work into all of the costumes and environments.... We looked at some cross-stitch, flatwork embroidery that Catherine of Aragon first brought to England, as well as some satin and Jacobian embroidery. Our director also referred us to the illustrations and paintings of Errol Le Cain, a prolific children's book illustrator and vital contributor to the look of Richard Williams's *The Thief and the Cobbler*. Henri Rousseau's paintings were similarly inspirational. They may defy gravity, but they give you a sense of space and environment."

"Initially, the suits we made for Lionel and Link evolved from looking at weaving and how it was just beginning to develop at the turn of the twentieth century. Weaving looms were coming into their own and could be a lot more experimental. The dyes and the colors were more vivid and becoming less reliant on natural pigments, and more synthetic colors were able to come in."

Cook and her team conducted intensive research to find out how to duplicate the warp and weft dynamics of real-world weaving in a smaller scale for the puppets. "We looked at many different versions of houndstooth, and it took us probably a year and a half of research to get the right size and colors," she says. "Overall, we created over thirty duplicates of the suit for Lionel."

Link's huge contoured body shape posed its own set of challenges for the costume department. "Computer-driven embroidery machines allowed us to consistently warp the plaid of his suit to wrap around his exact silhouette. This allowed frequent adjustments to the appearance without having to practically make many iterations," explains Cook. She adds, "The technology allowed us to program our hand-drawn designs into a sewing machine to embroider them for us." Digital precision was also a bonus in creating the multitude of costume duplicates. "It's really transformed our process as it frees up the costume fabricators to be able to work on crafting other elements."

"We wanted Lord Piggot-Dunceby's suit to look sharp and well tailored, which was challenging considering his round physique. To add to the expressive look of the suit, the fabric was also screen-printed with a subtle wood grain pattern to mimic moiré silk."

——— ANJA POLAND
COSTUME FABRICATOR

MR. LINK

ADELINA FORTNIGHT

SIR LIONEL FROST

FINAL PUPPETS

"INVEST WITH COLOR"

"NATURALLY OCCURRING PATTERNS"

GRANNY LINK

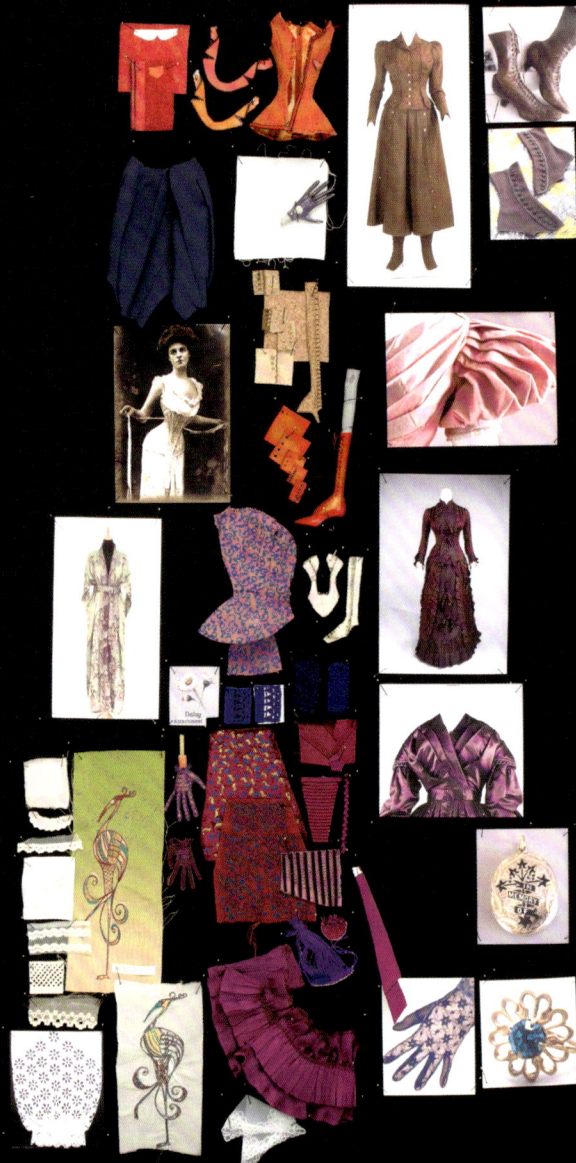

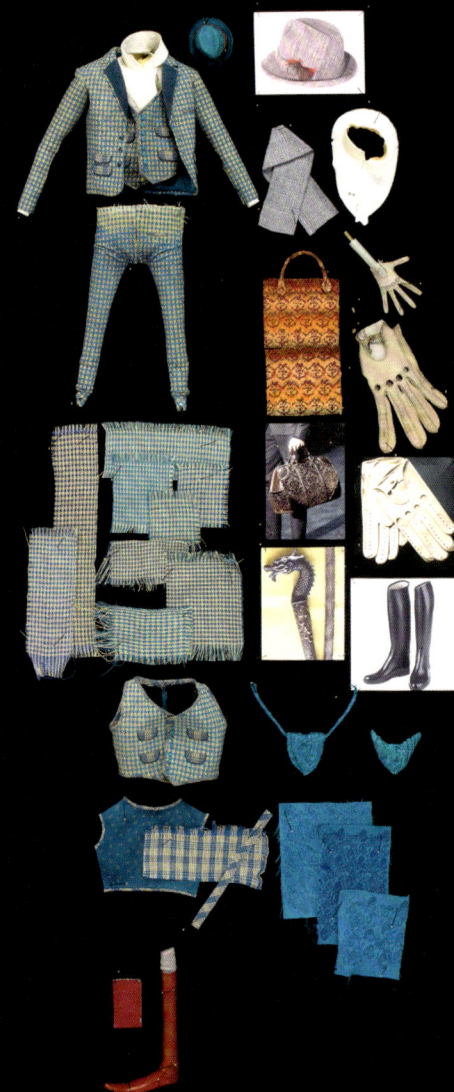

WILLARD STENK

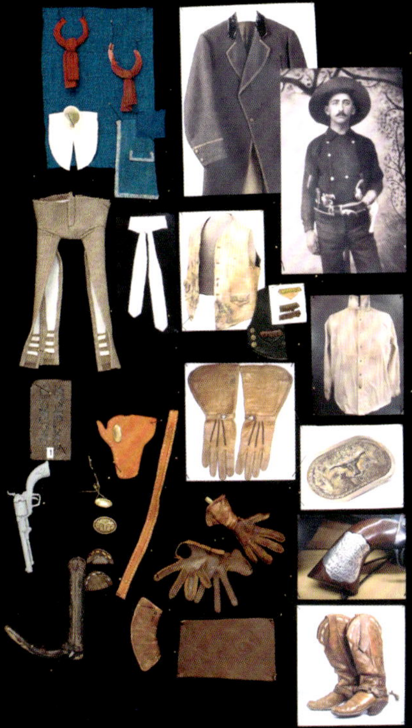

COSTUME DESIGNS

FUR COATS & SNOW BOOTS

PACIFIC NORTHWEST

HIMALAYAS

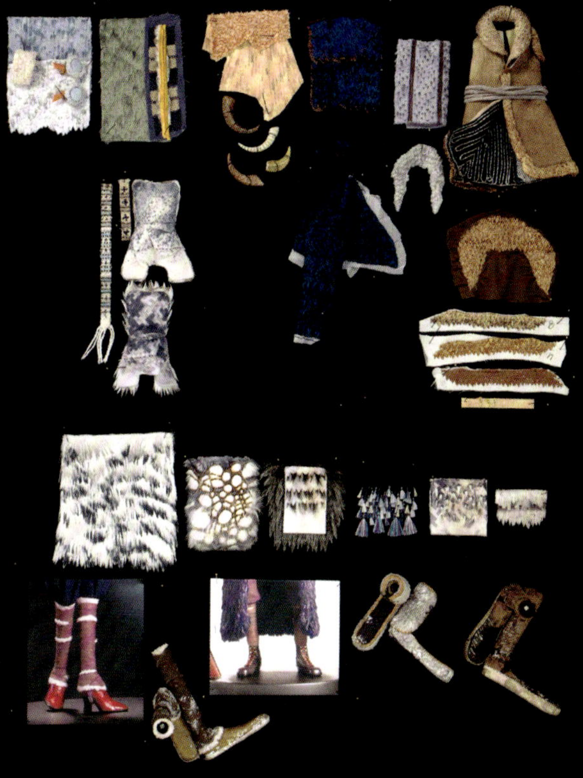

LONDON

OPTIMATES CLUB GENTS

MR. LINT

Costume Designs & Textile Reference Boards

2

LOCH NESS

◆

"Yes. Perfect spot. Now, we have work to do. Break out the bagpipes!"
—Sir Lionel Frost

Missing Link begins with our protagonist on an adventure close to home, relatively speaking, with Sir Lionel in pursuit of the most well-known mythical monster in Great Britain—Nessie, the Loch Ness monster. Aboard a rowboat on the loch, Sir Lionel and his unamused valet Mr. Lint lure the creature to the surface with a bit of music—but getting photographic proof of the encounter turns out to be a shade harder than expected.

◆

THE LOCH

Missing *Link* begins with a cold open set in Loch Ness, in the Scottish Highlands. Director Chris Butler wanted to suggest that Lionel had been monster hunting for a long time, so it was only natural that the audience should watch him pursue such a legendary creature. "When you think of the most well-known cryptids in the world, you think of Bigfoot and Loch Ness," explains Butler. "It felt right to begin the movie with a fun little trip to Scotland." The attempt to garner photographic proof of Nessie's existence quickly devolves into a thrilling rollercoaster-turned-rodeo sequence in which Lionel struggles to hang on to the famous Loch Ness monster.

When Lionel and Mr. Lint paddle out on the loch, it's just after sunset, a time the filmmakers referred to as *the gloaming*, and gorgeous deep pinks and lavenders reflect from the water's surface. Achieving the stunning look seen on film, however, came with its share of challenges—not least of which was how to approach the lake's water. "When you have elemental effects like water and fire, you want them to be stylized, but feel real as well. The water in the lake has to feel as real as Lionel's jacket," says Butler. Some early designs for the loch featured wildly stylized designs for the water with hard angles. "Gorgeous as it was, you just knew it wasn't going to be believable enough," notes Butler.

FIG. 1

PREVIOUS PAGES: Santiago Montiel

FIG. 1: Santiago Montiel

FIG. 2: Chris Butler

FIG. 2

FIG. 3

FIG. 4

FIG. 3: Ovi Nedelcu and Trevor Dalmer

FIG. 4: Max Narciso

FOLLOWING PAGES: Ken Pak, Trevor Dalmer, and Nelson Lowry

FIG. 1

FIG. 2

The task of achieving the believability and stylization Butler wanted required collaboration between art director Rob DeSue and visual effects (VFX) supervisor Steve Emerson and their teams. With thorough research of the loch's topography in hand, DeSue and his team first constructed a physical maquette of the environment, about the size of a dining table, out of craft paper and cardboard. The VFX team then scanned the maquette to add their own details and designs as they extended the set. "They could stretch and move hills around based on the composition. Every new detail was considered carefully," says DeSue. "We knew that this was the moment people were going to really take in the film's style." As the camera pans across the loch, the landscape is dotted with footprints—early hints to the movie's persistent motifs.

With the scanned maquette, Emerson was able to begin on the water, ultimately achieving the vibrancy, stylization, and realism seen on-screen. The result required careful attention to the reflections on the water. "We used a sky dome to get the patterning on the surface of the water," explains Emerson. "We were art directing the reflection of the sky, the sun, and the clouds—whatever was captured on the surface of the water." The elaborate patterning of the water established a motif that was carried throughout the whole film. "You see those same patterns in the clouds, the wood grain, even on the paint on the characters," notes Butler. "It's almost indescribable, but it's there, and you can feel it."

"Chris [Butler] said he wanted bold images with a large feeling of space and wideness. That's the kind of image I love to paint. One of my favorite paintings is Caspar David Friedrich's The Monk by the Sea, *and it's so rare to be asked in an animation feature film to express that kind of feeling."*

——————— SANTIAGO MONTIEL
CONCEPT ARTIST

FIG. 1: Trevor Dalmer
FIG. 2: David R. Bleich
All others by Santiago Montiel

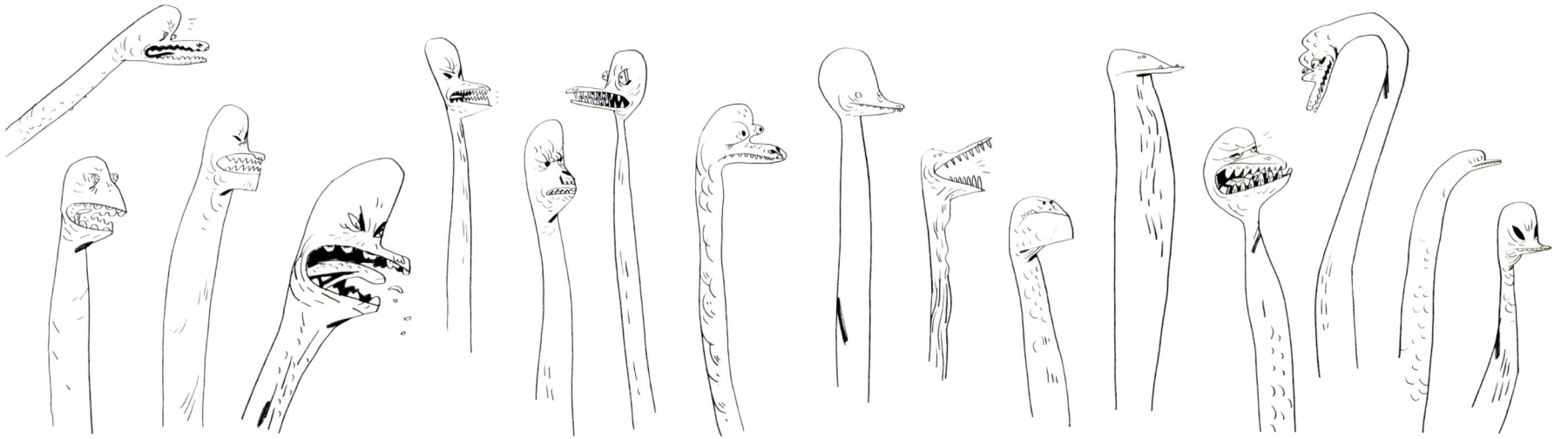

THESE PAGES: Warwick Johnson Cadwell

THESE PAGES: Ross Stewart

FIG. 1

FIG. 2

NESSIE

An offhand doodle helped establish the right look for the famous Loch Ness monster. "We tried so many different versions of Nessie, but we ended up going back to this ludicrous sketch I had drawn years earlier," notes Butler.

Butler's Nessie was definitely on the goofy side, but she was charming as well, with a glint in her eye. "She's essentially a balloon with an L-shaped face. But when you see her in the water, it's perfect. She is a combination of brachiosaur, whale, and seal." To refine the monster, character designers Warwick Johnson Cadwell and Juliaon Roels referenced endless images of prehistoric beasts and deep-sea creatures.

FIG. 3

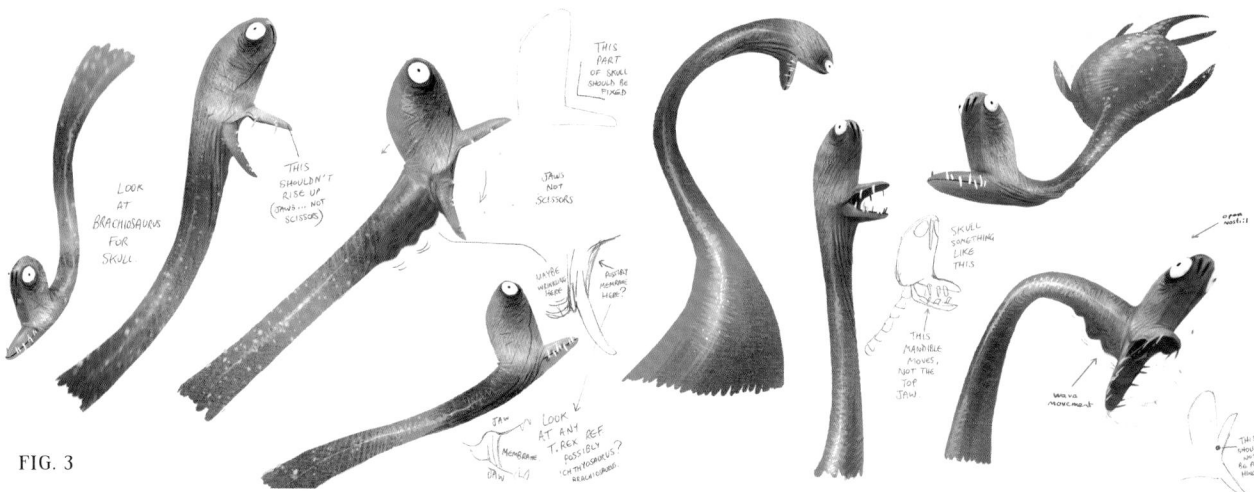

FIG. 4

FIG. 5

FIG. 1: Chris Butler

FIGS. 2, 3 & 4: Juliaon Roels

FIG. 5: Warwick Johnson Cadwell

FIG. 1 FIG. 2

CRAFTING NESSIE

It took sculptor Kent Melton over a month to build the main Loch Ness monster model. "She was about two feet tall, with a very long neck," says the veteran sculptor. "I used a polymer clay, which stays soft and takes art direction very well." Though the main Nessie puppet included barnacles, Melton was careful that the details wouldn't become too distracting. "The main thing about this model was that it needed to have a simple silhouette, and the designs were very playful."

FIGS. 1 & 2: Louis Thomas

"We wanted Nessie to have the feel of a Harryhausen monster but in the style and look of our film. The biggest challenge in creating [the CG] Nessie was the scale; the movement and look of the water running off of her when she is above water was particularly tricky."

——— ERIC WACHTMAN
CG LOOK DEVELOPMENT LEAD

THESE PAGES: Production maquettes sculpted by Kent Melton and Christy Becker

3

THE PACIFIC NORTHWEST

> "Dear Sir Lionel Frost. As famed seeker of mythical beasts, you may be interested in this proposition. I can reveal to you the as-yet-undiscovered creature known as *the Sasquatch . . .*"
> —Letter from Mr. Link to Sir Lionel Frost

With Mr. Link's letter in hand, Sir Lionel Frost boards a steamship to America and makes his way across the continent. In Washington State, on a little trail through the forest along Old Kemp Creek, lies the proof he's been looking for.

FIG. 1

A MEDLEY OF—— BLUES AND GREENS

Sir Lionel's quest to find the legendary Sasquatch takes him from London to the remote forests of the American Pacific Northwest. Blues and greens are the dominant colors of this lush setting, where we also meet Link, the mysterious and lovable center of the film. As production designer Nelson Lowry recalls, "The look and feel of that setting was a place that we knew, because we live in Portland. It's really my backyard, and I could just go out, look at the trees, and take pictures," he says. "We wanted all the trees, the ivy, the moss on the ground, everything to be authentic."

Lowry says that while the overall location style was easy to agree on, the actual task of designing nature for stop-motion was challenging. "You can look at a room and immediately notice that there's a chair, there's a table—but in nature, atmospheric perspective, materials, and scales are all huge issues. We had our trees growing and shrinking depending on what's behind the character."

Of course, one of the most crucial elements of the location is how it all fits in with Mr. Link. "He is such a strong element in the movie, he has to look at home in this background," explains art director DeSue. "The ivy on the trees, the way we manicured the grass, the way the branches looked on the trees were all in the service of making him look at home. Link had to look perfect in the clearing."

The color scheme for this sequence was heavily examined and considered. "The sun rarely penetrates the canopy of the dense forest, so the colors had to be rich and cool," says Lowry, who sought to highlight the bluish needles of the forest's Douglas fir trees in his artwork. Each new piece helped further the setting's rich blues, cyans, and teals, with the added aim of making sure Link, when he appears, pops on the background. "After many iterations, my first concept painting ended up with almost no greens," says concept artist Trevor Dalmer. "We knew we were saving greens and yellows for the Indian jungle."

FIG. 2

FIG. 3

FIG. 4

PAGES 58–59: Ken Pak   FIGS. 1 & 3: Trevor Dalmer   FIG. 2: Nelson Lowry   FIG. 4: Santiago Montiel   FOLLOWING PAGES: Trevor Dalmer

INTRODUCING
MR. LINK

FIG. 1

FIG. 2

The heart and soul of the movie is none other than the childlike and surprisingly witty Mr. Link (voiced by Zach Galifianakis), otherwise known as the legendary Bigfoot. Link's design was one of the most important components of the movie.

In order to pitch the film early on, Butler actually came up with a rough doodle of Link in his notebook. "Of course, it was finished more thoroughly to be more presentable, but so much was in the original sketch," he says. "We tried numerous artists to see where we could go with it, but no matter what we tried, people would come back to the original sketch and everyone said how appealing they thought it was. I heard it enough times that I thought, 'Well, I don't know. Maybe, there's something here!'"

FIG. 3

FIGS. 1, 3, 4, 5, 7 & 8: Chris Butler

FIG. 2: Juliaon Roels

FIG. 6: Warwick Johnson Cadwell

PAGES 66–67: Ken Pak and Nelson Lowry

FIG. 4

FIG. 5

FIG. 6

FIG. 7

FIG. 8

"Link's clothes had to look tight and restrictive but also move like he's in a leotard. His body had to be able to squash down, stretch up tall, twist, and turn, all while his shirt and waistcoat hugged his belly, which was a challenge since he's pear-shaped. We put in a series of elastic panels under the back of Link's jacket to allow for all this movement."

— COLETTE NICKOLA
LEAD COSTUME FABRICATOR

FIG. 1

MR. LINK: THE PUPPET

Standing about fourteen inches tall, Link was one of the largest puppets on set, so his construction and rigging posed many challenges. As John Craney, the film's puppet fabrication supervisor, explains, "Link was a furry character, but it's stylized fur—and there is some fairly complex geometry underneath the surface."

Craney says the Link puppet spent a significant time in research and development as the team processed numerous swatches and stylized fur panels. As animators constantly manipulate a puppet, the tiny and minute shifts on its surface will eventually accumulate with each frame and produce an undesirable effect called *crawl*—and with fur in particular, crawl is infamously difficult to avoid. "You have to figure out a material for the fur that will give you the look you need but will also have a memory and rigidity, or 'return,' to it," explains Jessica Lynn, hair and fur fabrication supervisor. The team tried folded, pressed, and sealed textiles and yarns, as well as sculpted and cast foam and silicone prototypes, to deliver the level of stylization required by the 2D designs.

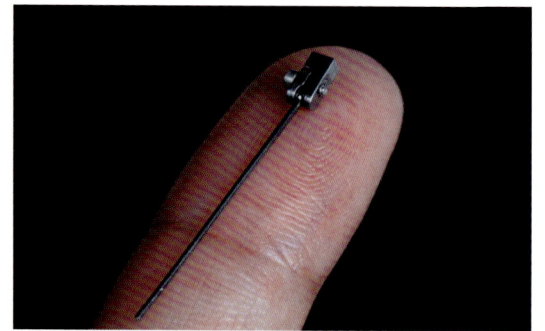

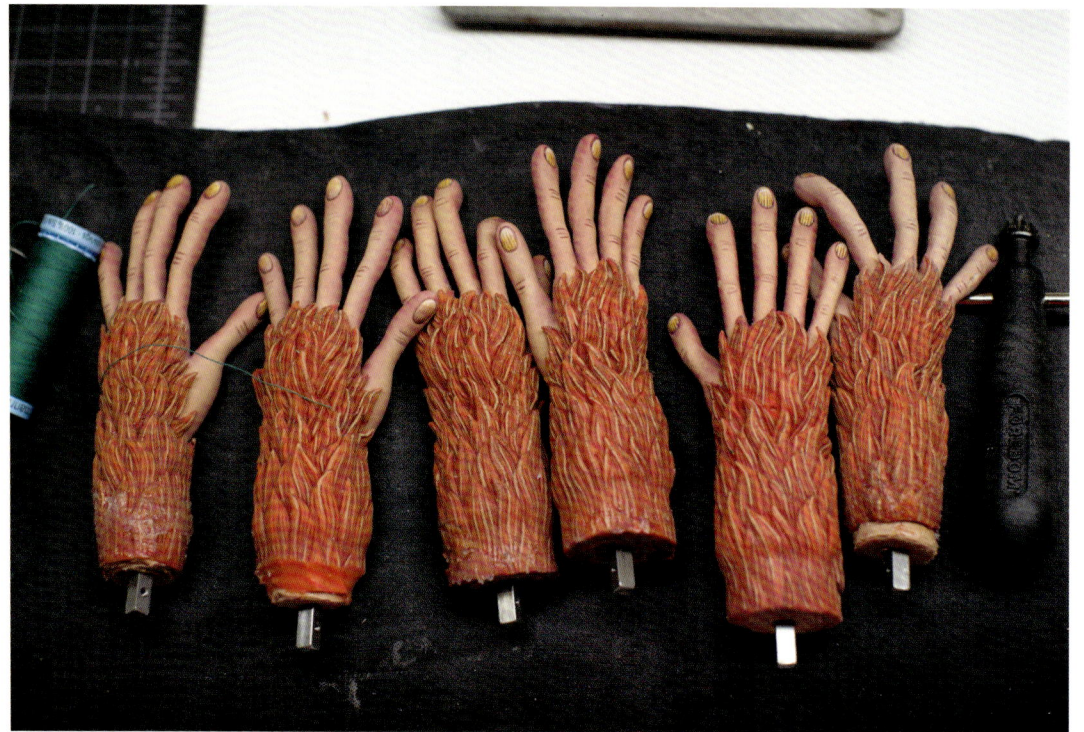

In the end, Link's body, arms, and legs were a mix of cast solid silicone parts and hand-applied silicone pelts, while his neck consisted of a cellular-walled foam cone that was able to compress and stretch with a range of movement similar to a slinky. Approximately five hundred individual urethane fur elements encompassed the puppet's neck and head.

The Link puppet was further enhanced by a host of additional internal mechanisms that aided Link's articulation and range. An internal chest breather, squash-and-stretch spine, and incremental belly mover helped animators achieve an anatomically credible performance.

FIG. 2

FIG. 1: Trevor Dalmer
FIG. 2: Max Narciso

ADVENTURES IN RAPID 3D RESIN PRINTING

Since its start in June 2005, LAIKA has pushed 3D printing technology to create the many different facial expressions required for its main puppet characters. "With every film, we have pushed the boundaries of what technology can achieve," says director of rapid-prototyping technology Brian McLean. "*Missing Link* is the culmination of almost twelve years of technology and know-how, and it definitely shows in the end results."

The movie marks the first time the studio is using full-color resin 3D printers for all its main puppets. Working closely with 3D printing company Stratasys and Fraunhofer's Cuttlefish software, LAIKA was able to take advantage of the possibilities of this new resin printer, which is more sophisticated and works differently than the powder color printers used previously.

"We let the creative drive the technology," say McLean. "I looked at the early character designs . . . and things like Lionel's sharp nose, Adelina's tiny nose and eyes, Link's facial designs—none of these things would be possible with the old printers. It would have looked like a completely different film with the powder printers. The powder technology had great color, but it struggled with fine feature details. The sharp angles were prone to breakage."

In total, over 103,000 faces were created for *Missing Link*: Lionel used 38,000 different faces, while Link had 25,500 and Adelina required 12,500 3D-printed faces. That's a huge jump from the 64,000 total faces that were created for *Kubo and the Two Strings*.

"In the previous movies, our animators used expression kits," says McLean. "We could cycle through them, and the faces would be reused for different scenes. But for *Missing Link*, we had our foot firmly planted in customization. Animators would create facial expressions specific to each scene. We had to get our process refined enough to handle that volume so we could deliver unique assets for every shot."

Looking back, McLean is thrilled to have been able to utilize the brand-new technology to deliver the characters just as Chris Butler had imagined them. "I never want to tell a director we can't create their vision," he notes.

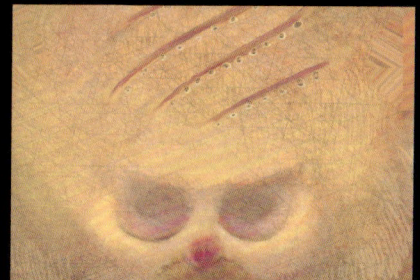

FIG. 1: Bizarre and beautiful unwrapped facial texture maps by Tory Bryant and Evan Larson

FACING REAL EMOTIONS

Facial animation supervisor Benoit Dubuc realized that the introduction of the new 3D-printing technology allowed him to really push the standards in terms of the characters' expressions throughout the movie. "This was my first movie at LAIKA, and I knew that the director wanted to really push nuance and subtlety of performance," says Dubuc, who has worked as animation supervisor on movies such as *X-Men: Days of Future Past* and *The Chronicles of Narnia: The Voyage of the Dawn Treader*.

In the past, Dubuc explains, computer-generated facial performances would be submitted and previewed only from the front-view camera perspective in isolation. "You block the face in and fine-tune it based on body performances," he notes. "It's one of the last things you touch when you create CG performances. What I wanted to do was marry the facial and body performances in this environment, so we decided to use reference video ahead of time to inform our facial performances. Whenever we could, we would ask the stage animator to provide a reference of what they'd be performing, even one month before the actual shoot."

Dubuc says this process allowed the facial animation team to be bolder with the complexity of the performances, favoring the performance to camera more than in previous projects. "We were able to provide the faces required for each scene with much more specificity as we printed them on a shot-by-shot basis, beyond a preprinted library of faces."

The initial meeting of Lionel and Link in the Pacific Northwest was one of the most challenging sequences for the facial animators. "It was one of the first scenes we attacked, and we had to define the characters and identify the range of emotions they were experiencing," he recalls. "We meet Link for the first time here, and we learn that he and Lionel share this loneliness. Lionel is a flawed protagonist who is not very self-aware, but he recognizes Link's feelings and surprises himself. We wanted to convey all of that not so much with dialogue but with facial performances."

For inspiration, Dubuc looked at everyday live-action footage to deliver LAIKA's trademark naturalistic and anatomically correct performances. "The challenge was taking this very graphic style of design and maintaining accurate facial anatomy," he notes. "For Lionel, we looked at Hugh Jackman himself—for example, the way his cheeks fill up when he smiles or his brows wrinkle when they furrow. Then, we had to simplify those lines to achieve the same sense of flesh movement, volume preservation, and musculature."

The team used ape footage to get references for Link. As Dubuc explains, "You can see it in the way his muzzle stretches out when he says the *oo* phoneme, the way his nose bends and flairs, and how his brow is a simple rigid ridge. That comes directly from ape references."

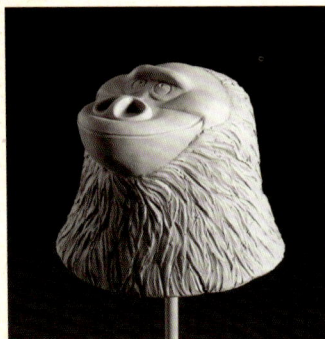

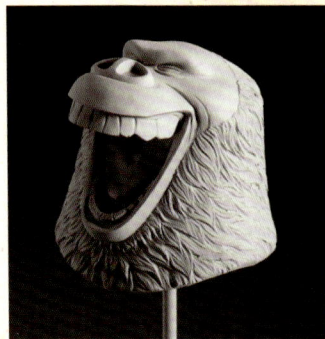

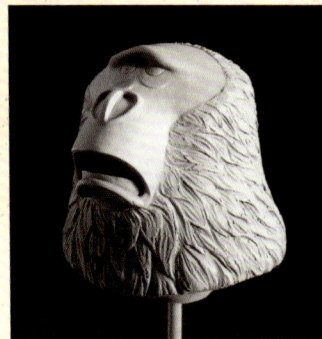

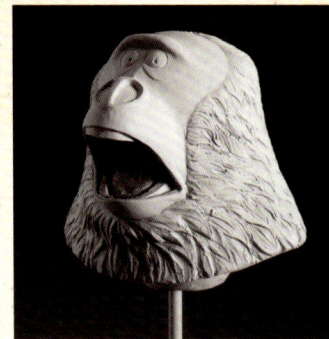

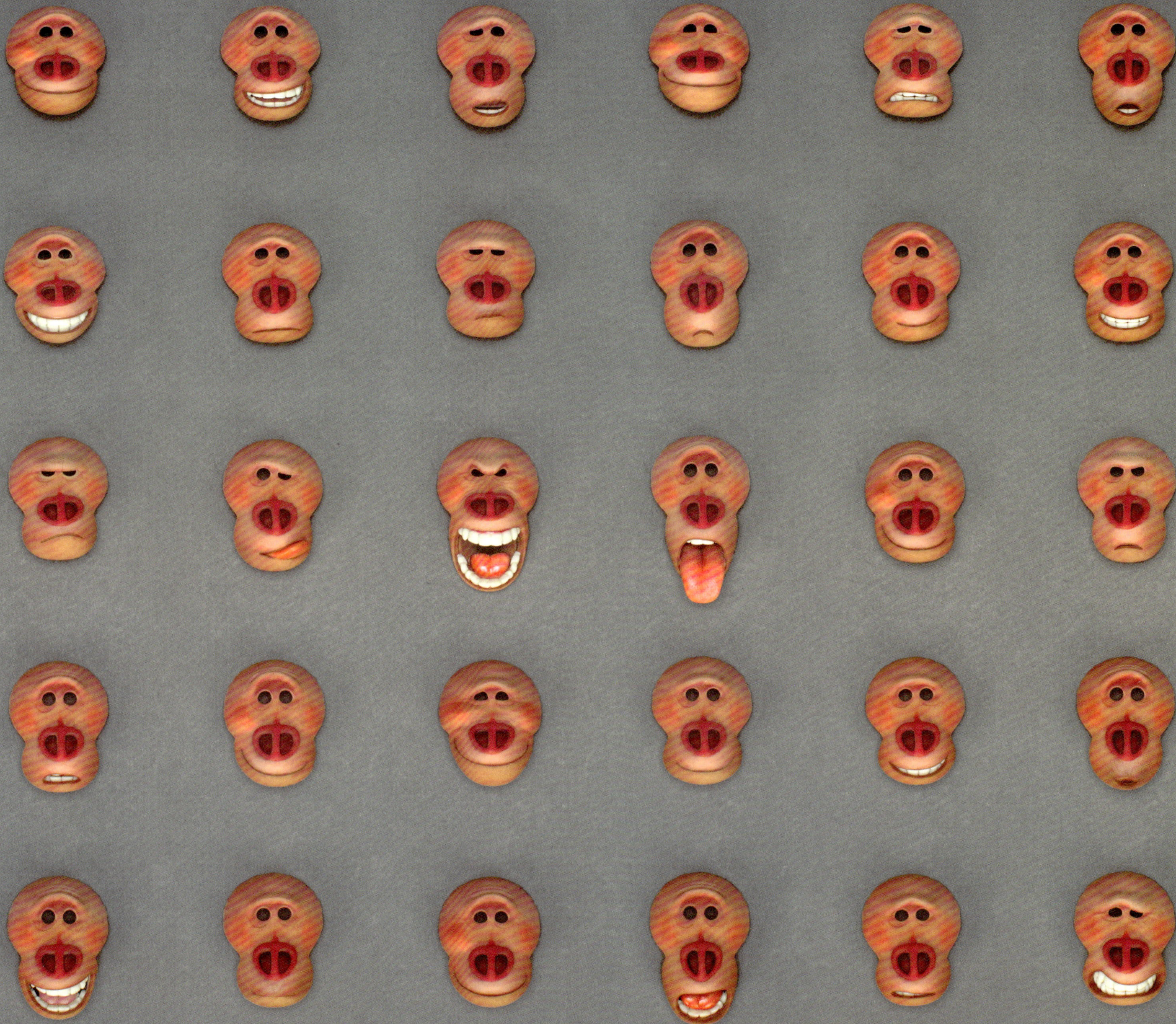

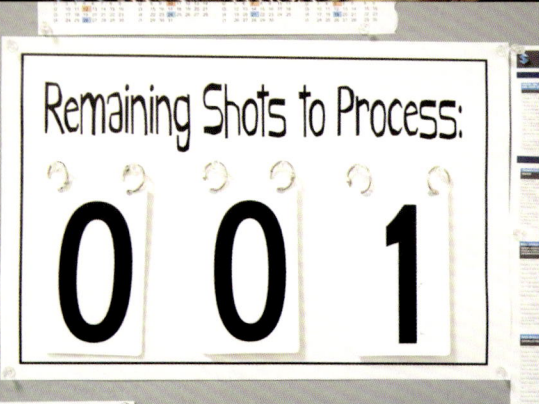

Remaining Shots to Process: 0 0 1

Green 1

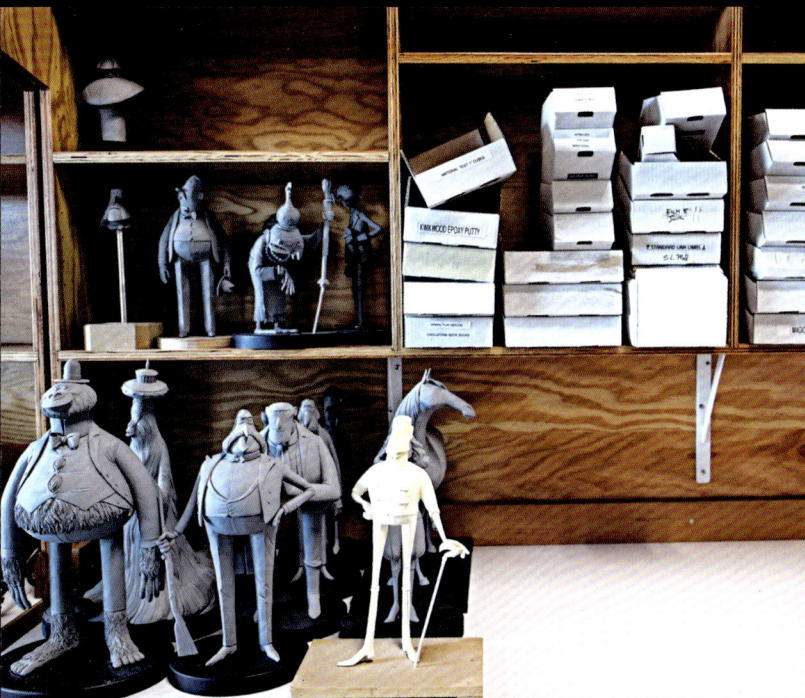

UNIT 1   UNIT 2
UNIT 5   UNIT 3
UNIT 6   UNIT 4
UNIT 7   UNIT 4.1

SIR LIONEL'S HORSE

FIG. 1

Says director Chris Butler, "Quadruped characters have traditionally been very difficult to realize as puppets, especially one with such specific musculature as Lionel's horse. It's all on show. You can't cheat anything. I was staggered by the stylized elegance and authenticity of the puppet that was created for this movie."

Puppet fabrication supervisor Georgina Hayns found inspiration in how the puppeteers of the stage show *War Horse* created their equine players. "Our team came up with this beautiful prototype, which was made in a similar way as *Missing Link*'s elephant for the sequence in the Indian jungle," recalls Butler. "Even the skin was created to show texture, and it was sculpted in a way to give the illusion of hair."

FIG. 2

FIG. 3

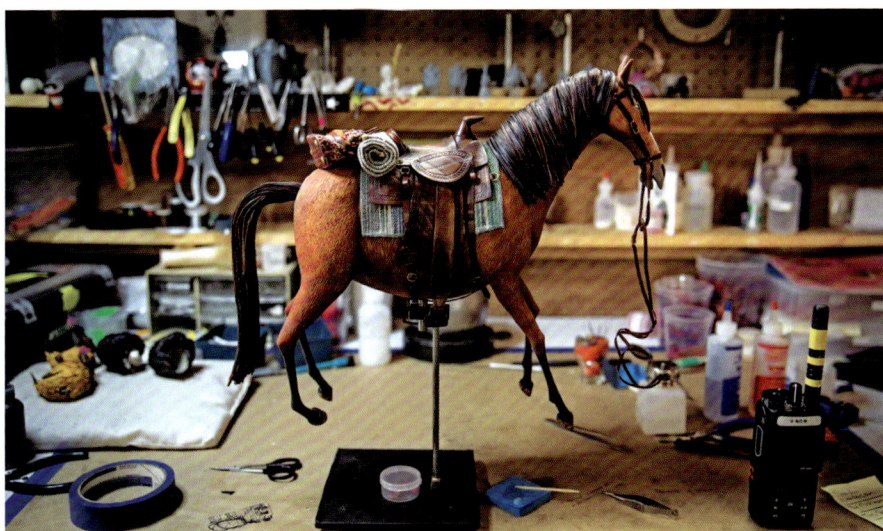

"The reins, bridle, and saddle were all made out of leather, with working miniature brass buckles. To achieve the required scale I had to skive (thin) the leather down dramatically, then wet mold it over the saddle form. The aim was to give the prop a luster and depth to enhance the tactile, real value for the big screen."

———— SHARI FINN
MODEL MAKER

FIG. 1: Juliaon Roels   FIG. 2: Trevor Dalmer   FIG. 3: Juliaon Roels and Trevor Dalmer   **FOLLOWING PAGES**: Trevor Dalmer and Nelson Lowry

McVITIE'S SALOON

We follow Lionel and Link to a rundown tavern in "the armpit of the Pacific Northwest," per the script. The bar is packed with rough-and-tumble patrons, who look up from their drinks as Lionel and Link pass by. The logging town contrasts with the urban sophistication of Lionel's high-society London.

"We knew McVitie's had to be gritty and downtrodden but not colorless," says Nelson Lowry of the intimidating bar. "We kept the color intensity to a comparative 60 percent and instead worked on wearing down the surfaces. Every wall, table, floor, and many of its denizens looked worse for wear."

Concept artist Santiago Montiel says he enjoyed digging up old photos of Portland and the surrounding region as research for this location. "It was my first time in the city, so I went to Powell's bookstore and looked at old books about the 1900s," he recalls. "You can always use your imagination to create the right ambiance and the characters, but when you are drawing a place based on real, historical structures, it's always best to look at real sources. I also loved using what I call the orangey 'Sunday afternoon light,' which is very nostalgic." The team ended up using five different wood grains for the set, embossing them in green so they would pop under the lighting.

FIG. 1

FIG. 3

FIG. 2

"The logging town was one of my favorite sets I have ever worked on because it combined an organic landscape with the rugged architecture of the Pacific Northwest rural logging community. It gave us an opportunity to use a miniature set to complete the entire town, because the set would have been too large to fit on our stages."

———— CARL HAMILTON
SET DESIGNER

FIG. 1: Santiago Montiel and Nelson Lowry
FIG. 2: Ken Pak
FIG. 3: Morgan Schweitzer

INTRODUCING

WILLARD STENK

❈

A thorn in Lionel's side is the diminutive, shady character known as Stenk. Like the other villains in the movie, Stenk reflects aspects of Lionel's character. Lionel, Piggot-Dunceby, and Stenk all collect taxidermy and bones, but for different reasons. Stenk collects them as trophies. His affinity for violence shapes his design—from the angry-looking hook nose that mimics the spurs on his boots, to the bear claw scars on the top of his bald head. "He uses his head as a weapon," Butler notes. "Like a *pachycephalosaurus* . . . those dinosaurs that head butt when they fight."

Stenk also has a bit of a complex about his size. "I wanted him to be very diminutive, and he is always surrounded by bigger henchmen," says Butler. "Like many of the characters in the movie, I wanted to give him a unique silhouette, and his is one of the weirder ones we came up with." Stenk's silhouette was the final piece of the puzzle for the nefarious character, voiced by Timothy Olyphant. "We have one of the most handsome men in the world voice one of the most disgusting, ugly characters in the movie," laughs Butler.

FIG. 1

FIG. 2

FIG. 3

FIG. 4

FIG. 5

FIG. 6

"Human locomotion is naturally intuitive for a human animator, but dogs move around according to a completely different set of rules. It was essential for me to study reference footage to build an intuition of canine locomotion. On top of all that, it was important that I deliver an emotional performance through the puppet. Misty has her own little character arc that has to shine through the technical aspects of animation."

— JAMES MENDOLA
ANIMATOR

FIGS. 1, 2, 3 & 6: Juliaon Roels

FIG. 4: Warwick Johnson Cadwell

FIG. 5: Juliaon Roels
and Morgan Schweitzer

PAGES 86–87: Santiago Montiel
and Nelson Lowry

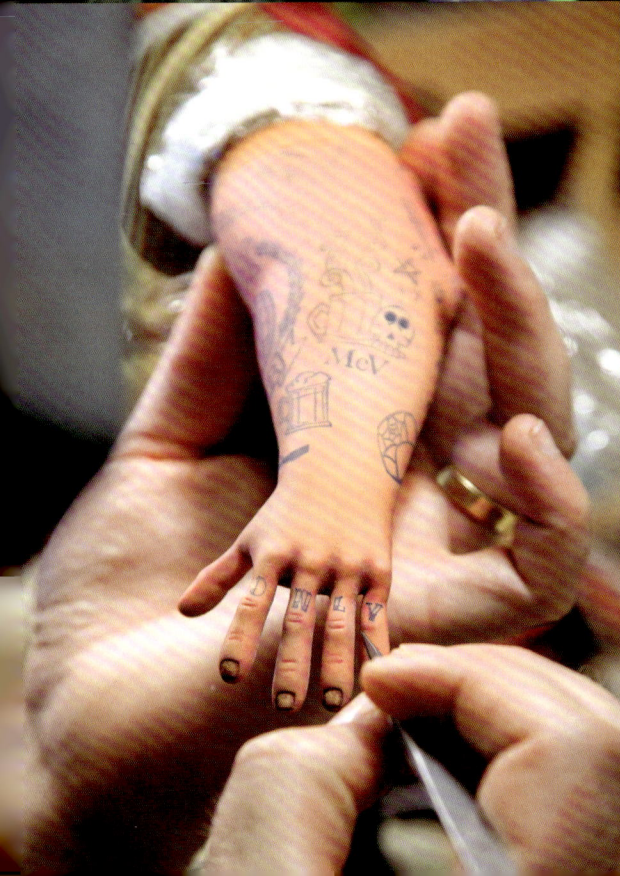

4
CALIFORNIA

❧

"You come here because you want something, and you think you can charm me and you can flatter me and I will do just as you say?"
—Adelina Fortnight

Mr. Link and Sir Lionel agree to a mutually beneficial arrangement. In exchange for scientific proof of Mr. Link's existence (in the form of a tooth, nail clippings, or feces), Sir Lionel will help Link find his relatives—the yetis. But the duo's only hope of finding the yetis lies with a map closely guarded by Adelina Fortnight. And Adelina and Sir Lionel have a bit of a history.

❧

INTRODUCING

ADELINA FORTNIGHT

✦

The movie's heroine is described in the screenplay as "part Gibson girl, part Amazon." Voiced by Zoe Saldana, the dynamic Adelina refuses to sit back and let the men in her life tell her what to do while they run off and have exciting adventures.

"I wanted a strong female counterpart to Lionel and wanted her to be an explorer in her own right," says director Chris Butler. "In her relationship with Lionel, I also wanted to cheekily hint at classic Hollywood romance but deliver something altogether different. Really, the movie is a romance between Lionel and Link. I took a lead from Sherlock Holmes's awkward and mostly undisclosed interactions with women to create this backstory for Lionel, where we knew he had a relationship with Adelina, but somewhere along the way it all went wrong."

FIG. 2

FIG. 1

FIG. 3

FIG. 4

PAGES 88–89: Trevor Dalmer
FIG. 1: Chris Butler
FIG. 2: Warwick Johnson Cadwell
FIG. 3: Dave Vandervoort
FIGS. 4 & 5: Max Narciso

FIG. 5

An earlier version of the script went into more detail about what happened between Adelina and Lionel. "Lionel and his friends and associates were hunting the chupacabra in the Mexican jungle, and so was Adelina," says the director. "They went on some adventures together, but she eventually married Aldous. The love triangle is implied in the movie, which helps sell Lionel as this flawed character who is not able to form relationships effectively."

As the film's producer Arianne Sutner points out, "I love the way Adelina wishes Lionel and Link well in the end and heads off to do something for herself. She is a true adventurer and unapologetic about it. She is a woman on her own, from another country, in a new world. There are lots of things working against her, but as an outsider she is very empathetic to Link. She understands because she has it a lot tougher than the privileged Englishman."

"I loved Adelina's dress and all its fiddly detail. Her collar was macramé with hand-dyed silk threads. The bustle was draped with stiffened interfacing that had a similar quality to paper towel. It's built in sections, each one we weighted, so that when Adelina squats down, the layers actually accordion down to the floor, and when she stands back up it goes right back to how it was."

—— COLETTE NICKOLA
LEAD COSTUME FABRICATOR

FIG. 1: Deborah Cook
FIG. 2: Juliaon Roels and Chase Nichol

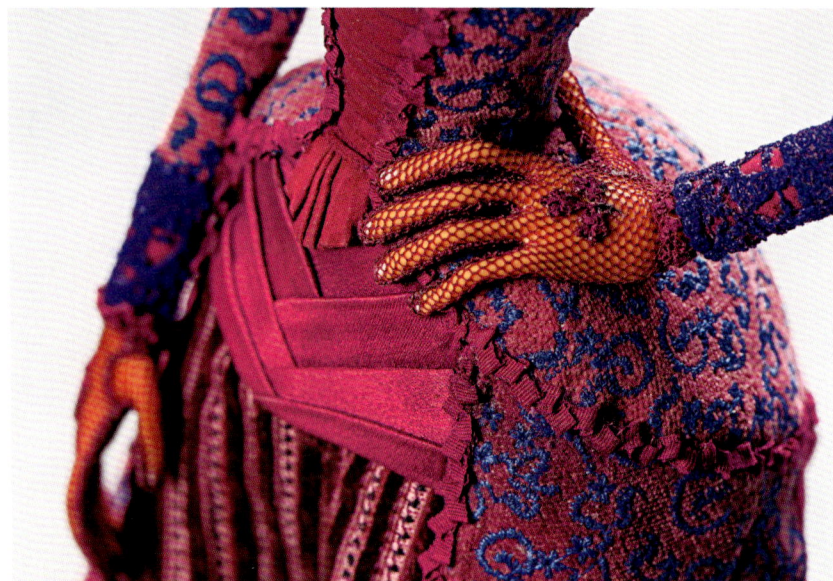

FIG. 1

FIG. 2

CALIFORNIA DREAMING: CASA DE FORTNIGHT

In Adelina's stately Spanish Revival house, the walls are punctuated with stained glass windows and the pathways infused with swirling mosaics. In the script, it's described as "more gaudy than Gaudí, but nonetheless a feast of vibrant flamboyance amid a courtyard replete with colorful cacti and showy succulents."

The heroine's home reinforces her state of mind, says art director Rob DeSue. "She is living in mourning and feeling imprisoned, so there's a caged-bird motif in terms of decor throughout the house. We have these strong vertical elements, these bars, all over. Even the way the posts and beams come together reinforces this idea of life behind bars."

Director Chris Butler says Adelina's sitting room wallpapers also contain a gilded-cage motif. "There's literally a bird in a cage in the scene as well," he points out. "One of the original concept designs had letters and papers on the floor, like paper on a cage floor. The beautiful stained glass window in the room streams the light from the tantalizing outside world." The motif pervades Adelina's environment: When Lionel first goes to meet Adelina, we see a swift flying free in the sky, and then the camera tilts down and we find her house behind the bars of a gate. Adelina also wears a broach with a swift on it, in which she keeps a photograph of her husband.

FIGS. 1 & 3: Santiago Montiel

FIG. 2: Santiago Montiel and Rob DeSue

FIG. 1

FIG. 2

FIG. 3

FIG. 1

FIG. 2

FIG. 3

"To bring the unusual cacti and succulent designs to life, we used a lot of custom-made and unconventional materials. We silk-screened and laser-cut craft paper, used textured fabrics, plastic beads, tissue paper, miniature railroad materials, goat hair, foam balls . . . To achieve the psychedelic color scheme, we used large quantities of black light paint."

—— *RACHEL OLSON*
LANDSCAPE ARTIST

FIG. 1: Andy Berry

FIG. 2: Juliaon Roels

FIG. 3: Warwick Johnson Cadwell

FIG. 1

FIG. 2

FIG. 3

FIG. 4

FIG. 5

FIG. 6

FIG. 7

FIG. 8

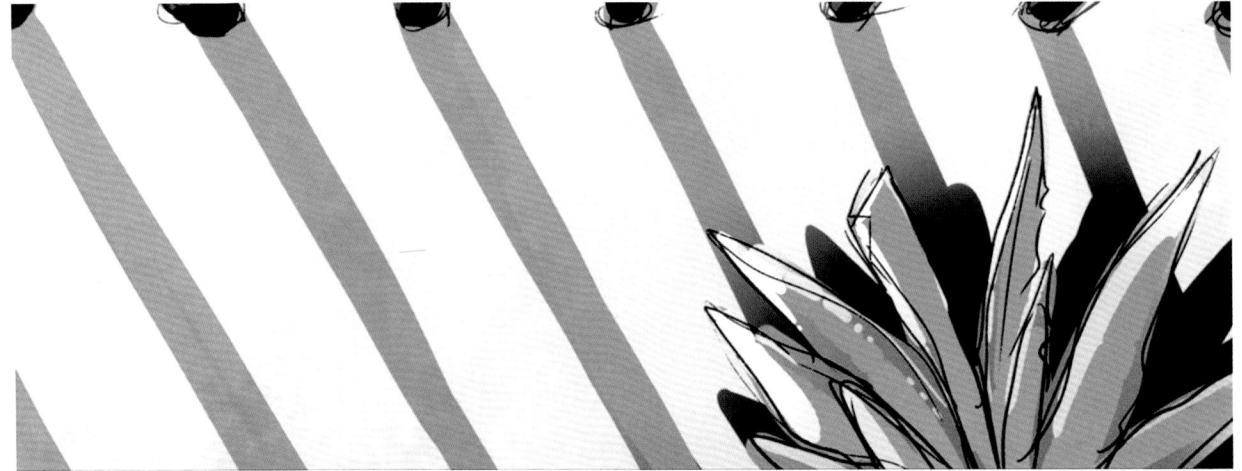

FIG. 9

FIGS. 1, 4 & 6: Brian Ormiston   **FIGS.** 2, 7, 8 & 9: Bridget Underwood   **FIG.** 3: Emanuela Cozzi   **FIG.** 5: Guillermo Martinez

FIG. 1

SANTA ANA TRAIN STATION

With Aldous's map in hand, Sir Lionel and Mr. Link make their way to the Santa Ana train station in disguise. But the furious Adelina sees through the pair's ruse immediately, and she's not the only one after them. A shootout unfolds between Stenk and Adelina as the others rush for cover.

The Santa Ana train is an intentionally stylized turn-of-the-century model. Lead model builder Raul Martinez notes, "When we were building the train, it was important that we stay true to the overall concept art but maintain functionality. Certain elements that are highly stylized can change the mechanical characteristics but give the final product a unique and distinctive look." Achieving realistic movement for the train meant mimicking actual train mechanics as much as possible and required crafting each element individually—whether by hand, machine, 3D printing, or laser-cutting.

Another challenge for the Santa Ana sequence was planning the shootout. "Just like in the heyday of Hollywood westerns, we had to carefully plan each bullet strike during the big shootout," says assistant art director Phil Brotherton. "Whether it was exploding luggage, a wood post, a trunk, or a suitcase, it was all worked out in the edit room before the first round was ever fired."

FIG. 2

FIG. 1: Santiago Montiel and Nelson Lowry

FIGS. 2 & 4: Warwick Johnson Cadwell

FIG. 3: Frederic Stewart

FIG. 5: Santiago Montiel

FIG. 3

FIG. 4

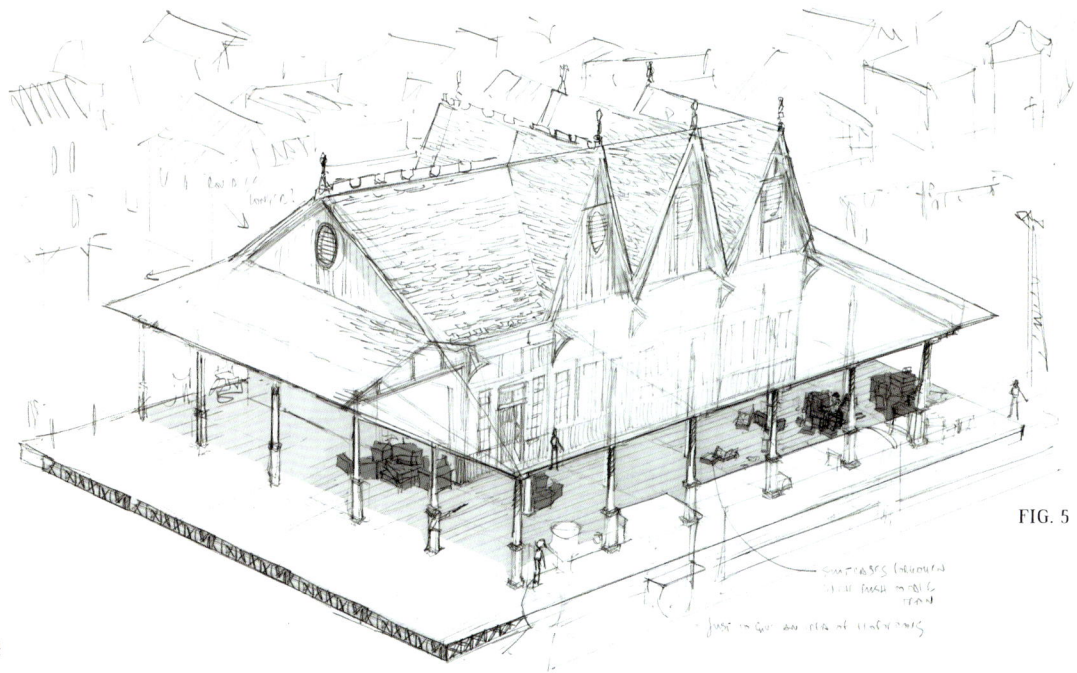

FIG. 5

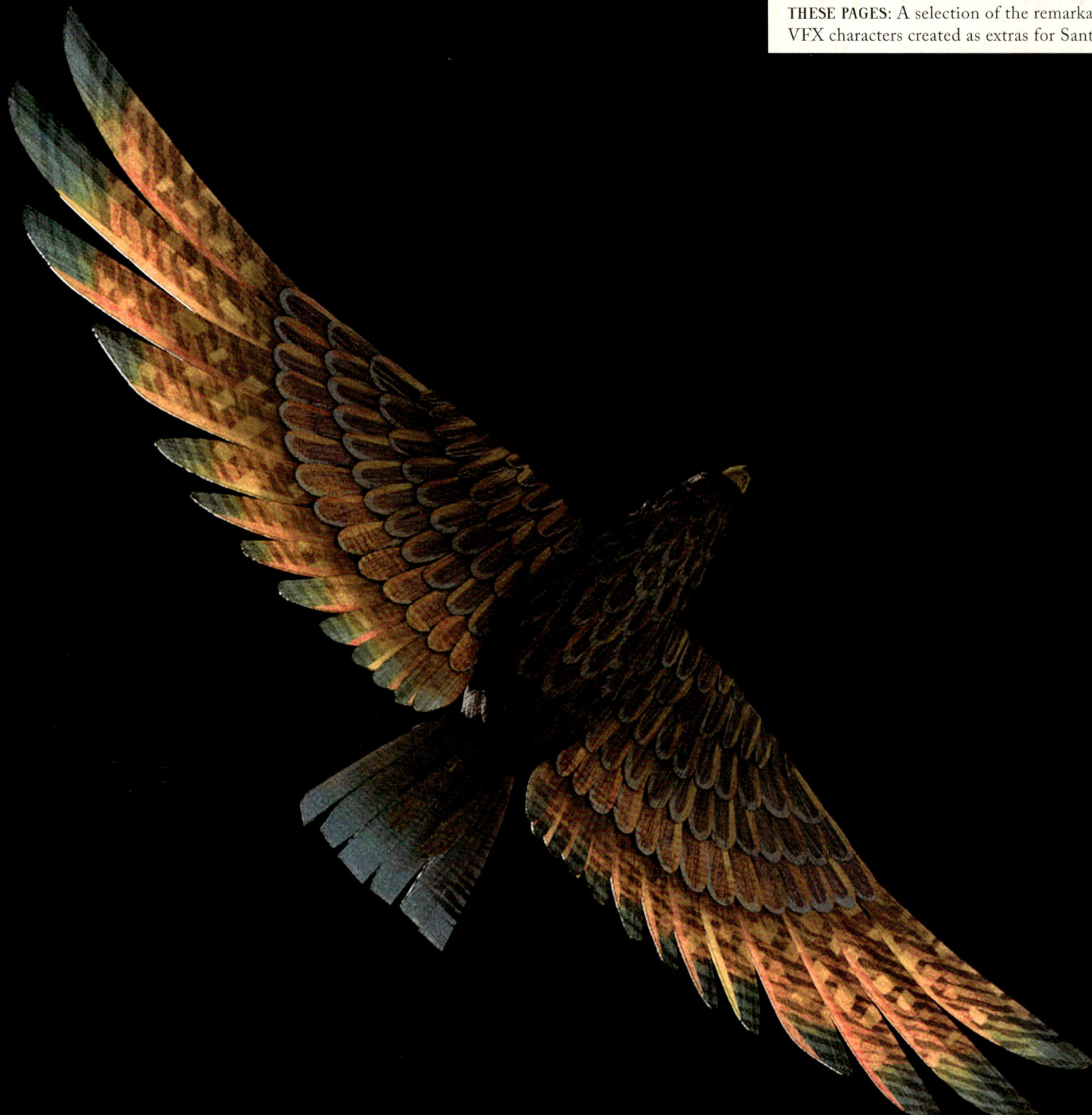

THESE PAGES: Side-by-side comparisons showcase the meticulous VFX artistry that goes into transforming practically shot elements into final movie frames

5

CROSSING AMERICA AND THE ATLANTIC

❧

"The hunter that follows us will not give up the chase easily. Do you understand? He's still on our tail, have no doubt. If he catches us, he'll shoot you dead, skin you, and have your pelt as his hearth rug!"
—Sir Lionel Frost

After escaping Stenk and his cronies at the Santa Ana train station, Lionel, Link, and Adelina head east to New York City and book passage on a ship that will take them to London.

❧

PUTTING A
STAGECOACH
IN MOTION

About halfway through the movie, Lionel, Link, and Adelina trek across the desert in a beautifully designed stagecoach. The set piece required months of planning and elaborate mechanical simulations to deliver the realism Butler envisioned.

As Oscar-nominated rigging supervisor Oliver Jones (*Kubo and the Two Strings*) explains, "We built the stagecoach with a three-axis rig to create the lateral movements of each puppet, and the puppets sat on top of a little ticktock rig, which we called a rumble seat." Since the bounce of the seat was programmed automatically, the animators could focus on the puppet performances. "This elaborate stacking of movements resulted in a very realistic impression of an old wooden-wheeled stagecoach rolling over the hard desert floor," says Jones. "However, the animators also had to deal with the puppets' jetpacks (rigs on the puppets' backs that enable the animators to realize minute increments of motion) as they were animating counter to the rumble seat." Assisted by a remote system developed by lead rigger Jerry Svoboda, the animators were able to access the puppet's jetpacks from the front of the stage.

PREVIOUS PAGES: Trevor Dalmer

FIG. 1: Rob DeSue

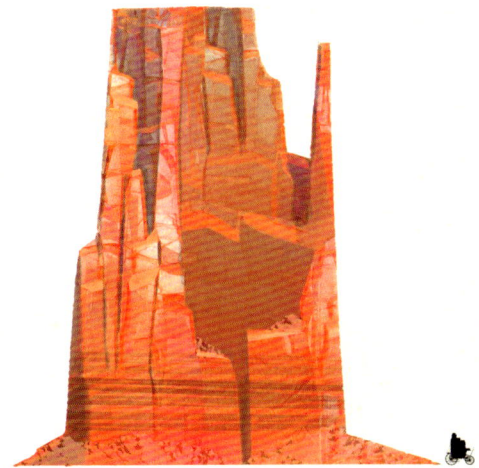

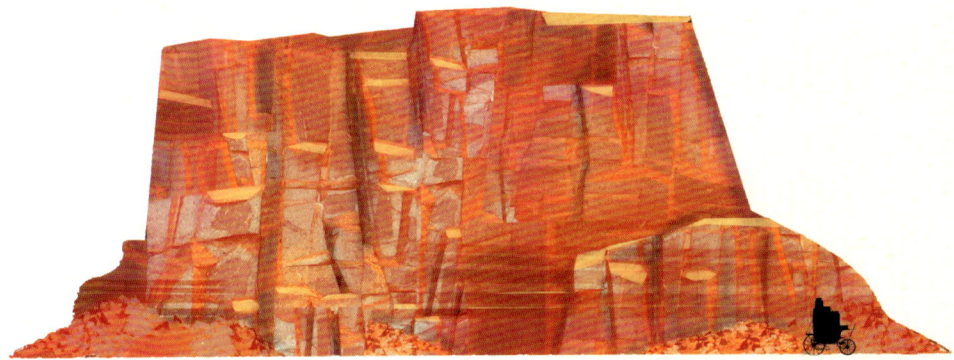

FIG. 1

Another mind-boggling detail involved the two hundred tassels that almost fill the entire frame of the coach interior. "So, you have this rumbling box that is about twelve inches wide by ten inches high, and inside of it, you have about two hundred quarter-inch-long tassels," says Jones. "We shot some reference and analyzed the movements of the tassels. Then, we hooked them up to a motor, which would move and add little bumps in the carriage motion."

Incidentally, the stagecoach was one of the first sequences Jones and his team shot for the film. "The build took about six months, from start to finish," he adds. "But it was one of the most detailed and enjoyable experiences of the whole picture."

THESE PAGES: Dave Vandervoort and Trevor Dalmer
FOLLOWING PAGES: Trevor Dalmer

FIG. 1

THE ——— NEW YORK CITY DOCKS

Butler and his team of artists and designers pored over old photographs, engravings, and illustrations of late-nineteenth-century New York City before setting off to re-create the city's docks. "It's actually very difficult to see what New York looked like in the late nineteenth century and early 1900s," says concept artist Santiago Montiel. "The cityscape changed very quickly in twenty years with the amount of buildings that went up." In the reference the team uncovered, they were struck by the bustle of people and how the sheer number of ships in the port created a dense crisscross pattern of sails and masts.

FIG. 2

FIGS. 1 & 2: Juliaon Roels
PAGES 116–117: Santiago Montiel and Nelson Lowry

THE
STATUE OF LIBERTY

I n the film, the Statue of Liberty is incomplete, sporting scaffolding and a mostly fresh copper cladding. Although historically the statue would have been less oxidized at the time, the artists opted for the statue to feature a blend of the original copper cladding and the iconic green patina we see now. "The Statue of Liberty is so iconic that it was a challenge to make a recognizable version that still fit into the world of the film," says look development artist Emily Neilson. "Her face went through a few rounds of alterations, but in the end I was really pleased with how her expression turned out."

THE
MANCHURIA SETS SAIL

One of the film's biggest action sequences takes place aboard a ship called the SS *Manchuria*—a nod to the ship that saves the hero from the mythical utopia of Shangri-La in the 1937 Frank Capra movie *Lost Horizon*, based on the novel by the same name. This dilapidated cargo ship takes Lionel, Link, and Adelina from the New York docks to London.

The sequence continued the film's unique emphasis on patterns and design elements. "It wasn't just walls and floorboards," recalls Butler. "It's about the application of paint, and patchworks and patterns of metal panels and pipes held together by rivets." Look development artist Emily Neilson explains, "For example, at first glance, the wooden deck looks brown, but the floor is actually printed with stripes of cobalt and blue ochre. This 'color-mixing' technique was one of several used throughout the film to pack as much color into one frame as possible."

The Atlantic crossing sequence involved a number of practical sets. A huge portion of the ship's deck was constructed, about twenty-eight feet in length, which represented about one-third of the full ship. The visual effects team then digitally built the rest of the vessel for set extensions and wider shots that reveal the boat being tossed around on stormy waters.

FIG. 1

FIG. 2

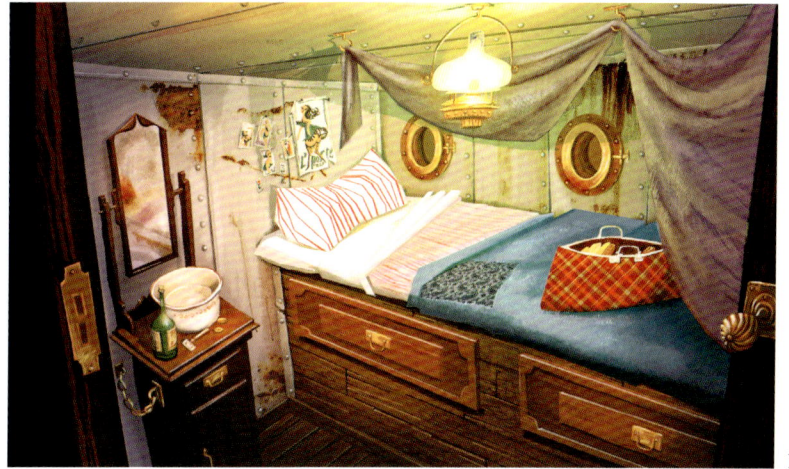

FIG. 3

FIG. 4

FIG. 5

FIG. 1: Juliaon Roels

FIG. 2: Juliaon Roels and Trevor Dalmer

FIGS. 3 & 4: Ross Stewart

FIG. 5: Ken Pak

FIG. 1

FIG. 2

As with the Loch Ness water, the ocean's wave patterns reflect the film's design motifs. "You'll notice a lot of angular shapes within the construction of the waves, as we wanted them to have their own signature look," says Butler. "Throughout the storm, we used a pattern of foam strips on the surface of the water, which we nicknamed the bacon effect. They used that in one shot for the storm sequence, and we liked the look so much that we asked for extra bacon for added patterns and textures all over the water surfaces."

Director of photography Chris Peterson says he and his team also had a lot of fun working on the chase sequence aboard the ship. "The boat set had a lot of tubes and hallways and we needed to figure out where to position the camera, how we could open up the sets, and how far the sets could be extended," he notes. "At times, the distance between the camera and lower deck walls was literally paper thin," notes lighting/camera lead Mark Stewart. To achieve the feeling of being with Lionel in the moment, Stewart avoided using green screens. He adds, "I wanted to see him being affected by the light as he ran through the ship, so we had to constantly remove and reinstall walls throughout the shot for the animator to work."

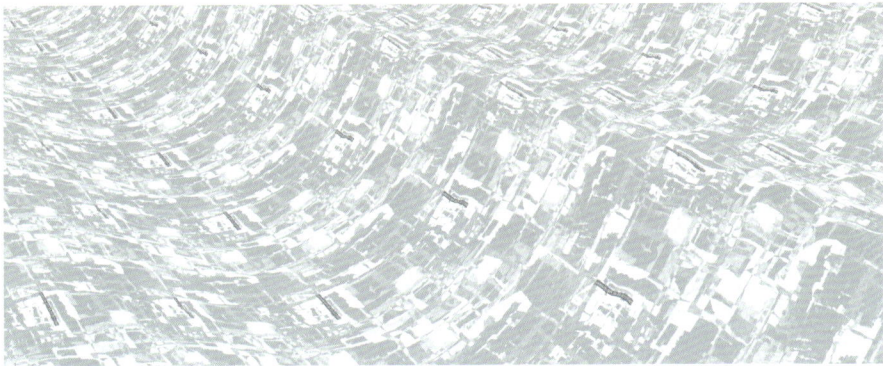

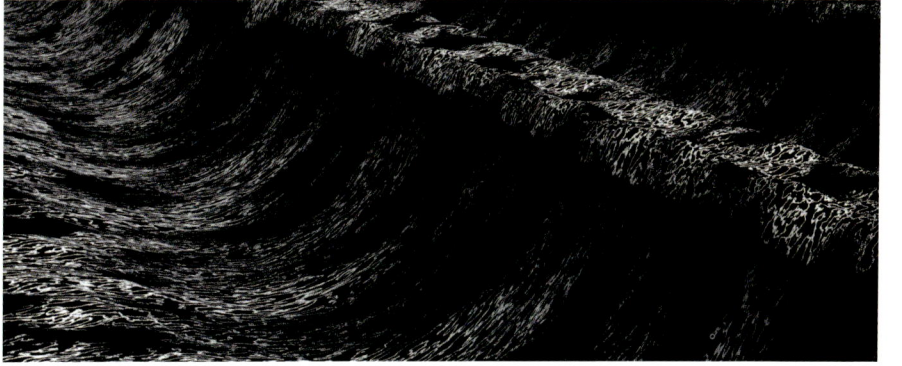

FIG. 3

FIG. 1: Ken Pak

FIG. 2: Dan Casey

FIG. 3: Early exploration paintings by Trevor Dalmer and VFX look development elements

FOLLOWING PAGES: Fiona Hsieh

6

ACROSS EUROPE AND INDIA

❦

Adelina: "This is just like old times, wouldn't you say?"
Sir Lionel: "Hmm, yes. Well, the Sasquatch is new."

Sir Lionel, Adelina, and Mr. Link speed their way across Europe and, mounted on an enormous elephant, travel through India. The lush jungle is a vibrant kaleidoscope of color. While everything seems perfect, the brutal Willard Stenk is hot on the trio's trail.

❦

FIG. 1

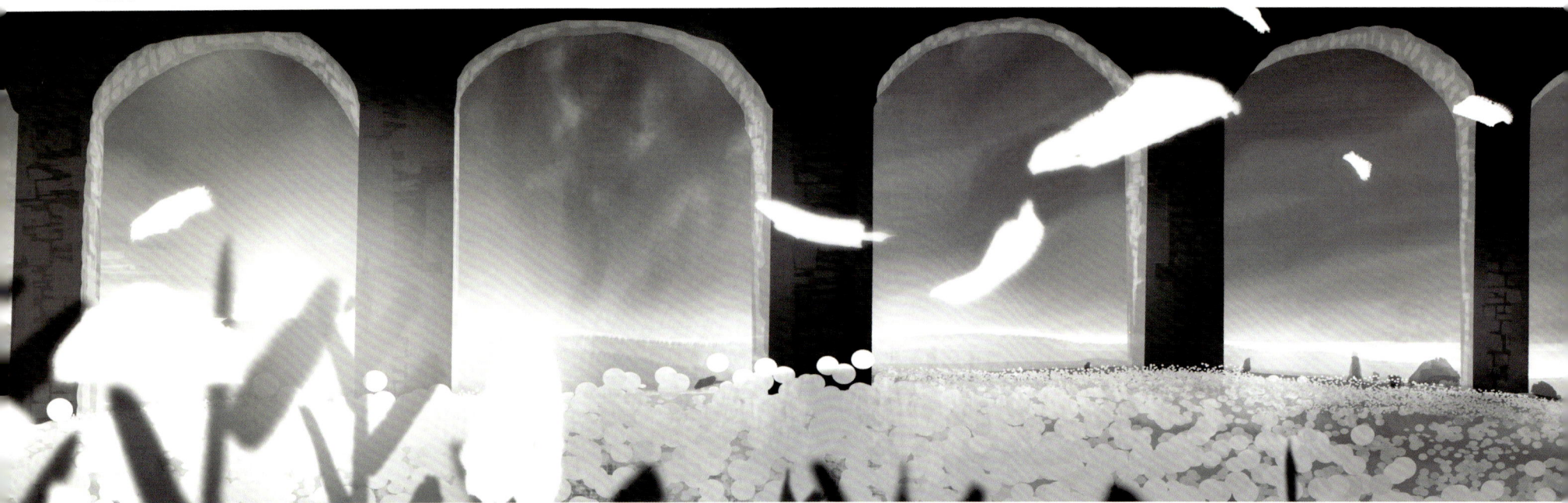

FIG. 2

TO THE COAST OF NORMANDY AND BEYOND

When Chris Butler first started to think about the movie's storyline, he knew that he had to find visual shortcuts to depict how his characters were traveling the world. He realized that he had a limited time and a handful of shots to cover a lot of ground, but he wanted those shots to be truly stunning. "I had seen pictures of the Pink Granite Coast of Normandy, along Brittany, and thought they were stunning. I wanted to choose specific locations and imagery that were memorable and established the right mood and sense of place."

Continuing through Europe, Butler picked a trip across a viaduct to continue paying homage to the powerful photographs seen in the pages of *National Geographic* magazine. The design itself is quite simple—a miniature viaduct, a

few trees, and a beautiful blue sky, created by CG matte painter and texture artist Joe Beckley, based on initial illustrations by Santiago Montiel.

The sequence also showcases several stunning changes of perspective—top-down shots that are more graphic than those taken by cameras at an angle. "These shots are slightly more designed and less photo-realistic, but they provide an epic feeling, and again, hint at the amazing scope of our characters' journeys."

Butler also makes extensive use of a classic adventure movie device: "Everyone remembers the animated dotted line from the Indiana Jones movies," explains the director. "We wanted to give it an additional dimension. We thought, 'Let's show Lionel's hand mapping out their course.' We got to see the animation of these 200 percent scale hands, as well as the props, which included

FIG. 3

a ruler, a pen, and a plate of Butler's Buttermilk Biscuits! In the end, it turned out to be quite an elegant, lovely scene which offered a lot of information in a relatively economical way."

The creative team storyboarded a few other locations for this scene that were too elaborate to produce efficiently. "Originally we had them sailing across the Red Sea on a dhow, and Lionel and Link were sitting on these bags of pistachios, pointing out to the stars in the night sky," recalls Butler. "We even got to see them sail past some camels in the foreground, which would certainly add to the epic feel of the sequence. It was a fun moment, but in order to keep the movie chugging along at the desired pace, some ideas inevitably fall by the wayside."

FIG. 1: Santiago Montiel

FIG. 2: Santiago Montiel, Trevor Dalmer, and Nelson Lowry

FIG. 3: Joe Beckley

THESE PAGES: Santiago Montiel and Ken Pak

FIG. 1

THE INDIAN JUNGLE

Because the film takes Lionel, Link, and Adelina to the deep jungles of India, it was only natural to have them travel on a magnificent elephant. "The scene in India is very brief, but it's here we see this group of misfits starting to bond together," says director Chris Butler.

The lush jungle setting provided an opportunity for the filmmakers to play with bright, tropical, fruity colors. Production designer Nelson Lowry produced a lot of the artwork that inspired the jungle sequence. "Everyone knows what a jungle looks like, but we wanted it to have its own level of naturalism," he notes. Lowry likes to call this process *Frankensteining*, by which artistic license is applied to real-world influences. "We looked at numerous photos of plants that grow in Indian jungles, and then we'd use as few as three or four main textures to represent the whole jungle."

Shey Phoksundo -

FIG. 2

FIG. 3

FIG. 4

FIG. 1: Trevor Dalmer

FIG. 2: Nelson Lowry

FIG. 3: Santiago Montiel

FIG. 4: August Hall and Nelson Lowry

FOLLOWING PAGES: Nelson Lowry

FIG. 1

FIG. 2

"I wanted the Indian jungle to feel quite alive and show a relationship between the natural environment and the ruins that is harmonious. Maybe we don't know which came first, the old stone structures or the jungle."

—— *WARWICK JOHNSON CADWELL*
CHARACTER DESIGN AND CONCEPT ILLUSTRATION

FIG. 3

FIG. 4

FIG. 7

FIGS. 1, 2, 3 & 4: Warwick Johnson Cadwell

FIG. 5: Juliaon Roels

FIGS. 6 & 7: Santiago Montiel

Lowry also points out that they made the vegetation in the scene transparent so that lighting would filter down, thus creating a humid green light. "We used material that had wax in it so we could get this special transparency, which was quite opposite of the dry woods in the Pacific Northwest sequence."

The jungle also provided interesting challenges for the rigging team, which had to accommodate a giant elephant and the massive trees. As director of photography Chris Peterson points out, "Because of the size, scope, and depth of the environment, the jungle sequence also involved a lot of planning. We had a lot of foliage in the foreground and the background, which is always a challenge in stop-motion."

Peterson said because everything had to be built on the stage and included in camera, they ended up shooting multiple layers for the scene. "Thanks to digital technology, we would shoot the elephant going through his animation path, and then we would focus on the environment," he notes. "This was all done on the same stage, but shot at different times to allow us to put everything together. We needed to make the scene accessible for the animator, as well as the motion-control rig to support the elephant. We needed space for our rigs and we had to fly cameras around it. The big puppets like the elephant or Lionel's horse need a lot of support to hold them up and move them through space. That's why we found ourselves shooting things as elements, even when they were on the same stage, and combining them later. It was quite challenging, but all worth it in the end."

THE ELEPHANT

The glorious elephant that carries our trio through the Indian jungle is one of the film's most impressive puppets. Over three feet tall, the mammal has rich, colorful fabrics on its back that stand out against the deep greens of the sequence. "It's all saying, 'Look at how grand this adventure is,'" notes director Chris Butler.

"We proposed an approach to the fabrication of the puppet that would hint at a stylized bone-and-muscle understructure, which would circumnavigate any sense of a locked-in, solid, static puppet when in motion," says puppet fabrication supervisor John Craney. The resulting elephant puppet's skin was capable of stretching up to 30 percent in some areas. Tethered to the armature at minimal positions, it could successfully collapse, hang, and ride over hip and shoulder bones.

FIG. 1

FIG. 2

"A big challenge with animating the elephant was finding the right gait for her unusually long legs so it would fit with the motion and speed of her body. I used footage of real elephants as a guide for the animation but as our character came to life, I left the live-action behind and instead started building upon successful animation tests, keeping the spirit of a real elephant but creating a unique walk for this beautiful long-legged creature."

—— BRIAN HANSEN
ANIMATOR

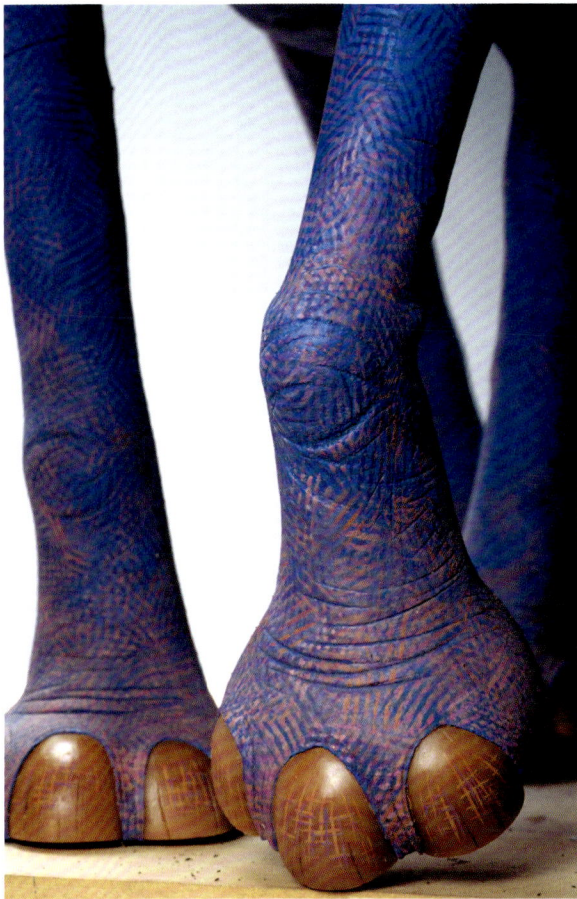

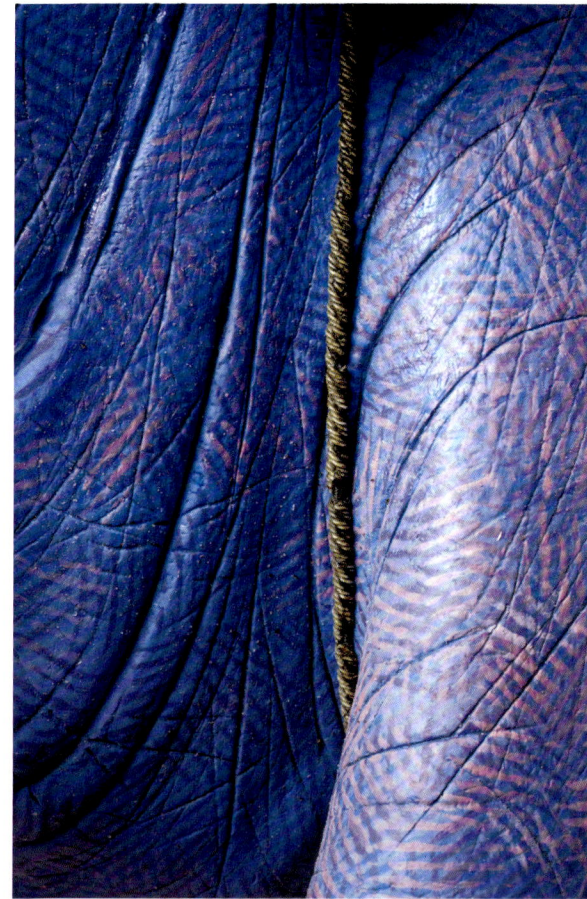

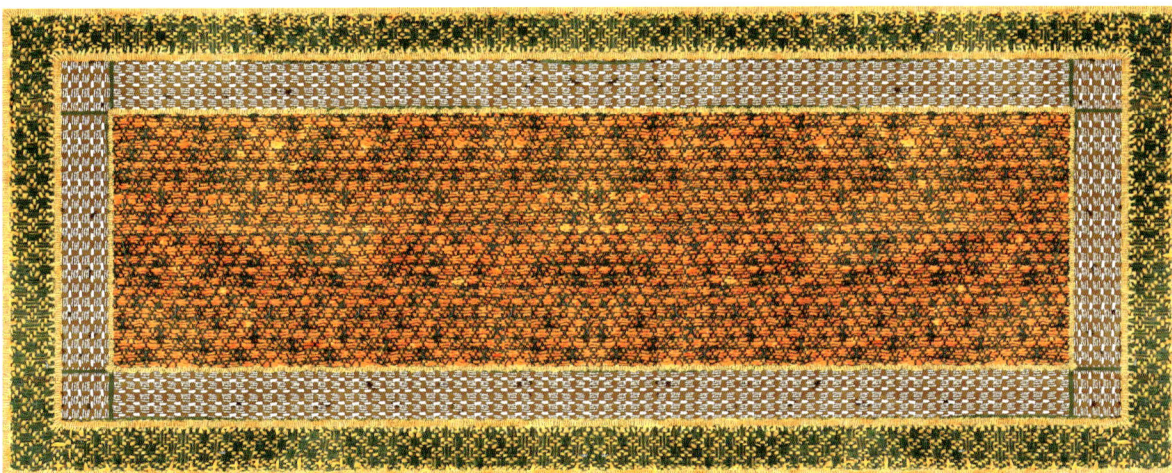

FIG. 1: Warwick Johnson Cadwell

FIG. 2: Juliaon Roels and Trevor Dalmer

FIG. 1

"There were a couple of shots that had very dynamic camera moves. As perspective changes throughout the move, the set needs to look fully realized in every direction we are seeing. This requires a considerable amount of depth. Rather than build a set the size of a basketball court, we shot the set parts in bus-sized sections that were reconfigured between passes."

—————— *NICK MARIANA*
LEAD SET DRESSER

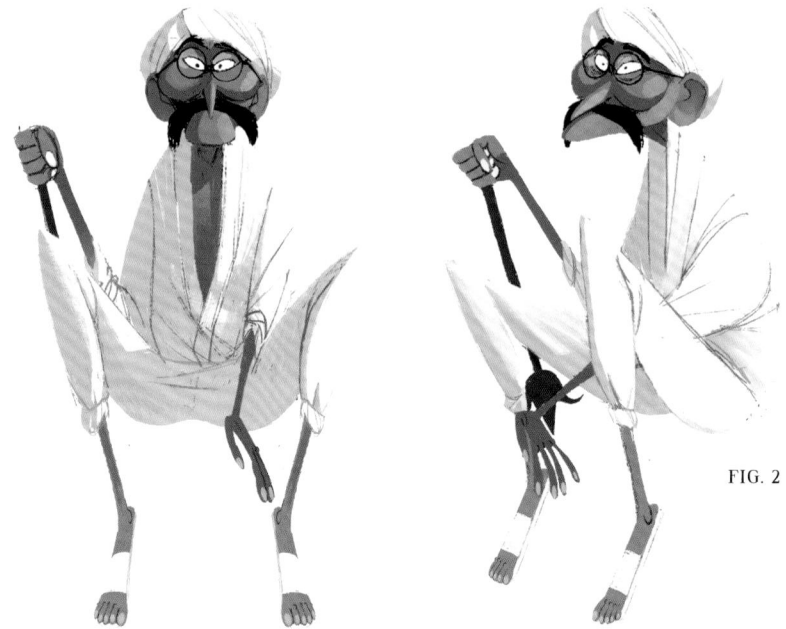

FIG. 2

FIG. 3

Puppet fabrication supervisor Georgina Hayns explains, "Like everything else in the movie, the elephant had to reflect the film's rich color palette and graphic style, as well as showcase naturalistic skin and textures." Hayns, who has worked on all five LAIKA movies, says the production valued realism in every element regardless of screen time. "The elephant is only featured in the movie for about three minutes, but we really wanted to capture the way his skin moves over his bone structure, over the armature and muscular sculpture."

Hayns says while the art department was working on the grass and the leaves, she and her team focused on the elephant's skin, hair, and fabric. Overall, it took the team about eight months to build, including R&D.

"We worked with styrene to sculpt the early abstract textures and molded them during the long development period, and eventually we came up with a highly stylized version of the skin," adds Hayns. Creating the baggy quality elephants have around their joints was a challenge. "We created flat sheets of soft silicone rubber and observed how the material would move on the elephant's feet," explains Hayns. "The material would crease and move nicely with the armature underneath it."

FIG. 1: Warwick Johnson Cadwell

FIGS. 2 & 3: Juliaon Roels

FOLLOWING PAGES: Nelson Lowry

7
THE HIMALAYAS

"The place you seek is not lost. It is hidden. Hidden by choice. Perhaps it is the men who seek it who are lost."
—Gamu

Traversing India and Nepal, the traveling companions make their way to the snowcapped peaks of the Himalayas, and begin their search for the lost valley of Shangri-La, home to an ancient civilization of yetis.

INTO THE MOUNTAINS

Of course, in a movie about an adventurous cryptozoologist in search of yetis, the third act must end in the Himalayas! Again, the film's artists dove into months of R&D to replicate the stark beauty of the white-capped Himalayan peaks.

"Our director was emphatic that this sequence should feel quite different, but also be influenced by the same stylistic approach," says production designer Nelson Lowry. "We probably had close to ten establishing shots for the Himalayas, and each one had to be striking. These shots start with the approach to the village past Gamu's residence and further on those mountains. For each shot, we had to figure out the amount of snow that had to increase with the altitude, as well as the change in colors and lighting."

FIG. 1

FIG. 2

FIG. 3

FIG. 4

FIG. 1

Lowry revisits Butler's vision of creating these grand vistas and the epic, vintage vibe of old *National Geographic* photography: "All of this would lead to the grand temple of the yeti tribe, which had to pack even more of the wow factor. Once you get into snowdrifts and mountains and weather particles, it gets harder to stay true to nature while adhering to all the stylistic elements. It really required using all the tricks I had in my repertoire."

FIG. 1: Santiago Montiel

FIG. 2: Nelson Lowry

FIGS. 3 & 4: Ken Pak

PAGES 148–149: Santiago Montiel

FIG. 2

FIG. 3

FIG. 4

"We wanted each vista along the Himalayan journey, from the rolling foothills to the peak of Shangri-La and everything in between, to feel visually different yet still a part of one world. We would digitally block out rough shapes and uniquely compose each shot in an effort to achieve visual variation. We then used common show patterns, materials, textures, and displacement techniques to unify the world."

—————— JOE BECKLEY
TEXTURE ARTIST AND MATTE PAINTER

WHITE LIGHTS, STUNNING HEIGHTS

For director of photography Chris Peterson and his crew, the Himalayas and yetis' temple sequence was one of the film's toughest environments. "Unlike many of the other settings of the movie, we were lighting an environment that doesn't really exist in the real world," he notes. "We were also dealing with snow and the compression that you have in high altitudes."

Aided by LAIKA cameramen John Ashlee, Dean Holmes, and Frank Passingham, and lighting/camera lead Mark Stewart, Peterson used twelve-by-twelve white reflecting bounce cards to re-create the way actual snow-covered mountains react to sunlight. "We had about six or seven units shooting the Himalayan sequences, and we had to be constantly aware of continuity," says Peterson. "It was a look that was quite different from our previous movies, which were darker in tone. We definitely had more white ambient light to play with in the snowy sections."

In their planning, Peterson and his team were assisted by detailed visuals storyboarded by Oliver Thomas and the director. "This sequence was easily the most complicated sequence I'd ever boarded," notes Thomas. "I'd done epic action sequences before but never something that, in addition to the straight action, layered on complex action, humor, and precise choreography to this degree." Though the task seemed daunting, Thomas and the director quickly went over the beats and choreography in minute detail at their first meeting. "Fortunately, Chris is a stellar board artist, so we were speaking the same language and had a pretty accurate idea of what was going to happen moment to moment," says Thomas. "The detailed planning, ironically, gives you the latitude and confidence to add little touches, and go down little tangents here and there that aren't in the script."

FIG. 1: Clement Dartigues

FIG. 2: Trevor Dalmer

FIGS. 3 & 4: Santiago Montiel

PAGES 152–153: Oliver Thomas

FIG. 1

FIG. 2

FIG. 3
FIG. 4

ADELINA, COULD YOU PLEASE TELL SIR LIONEL TO STOP SWINGING QUITE SO MUCH? HE'S MAKING...

IT IS VERY DIFFICULT FOR HIM DOWN HERE...

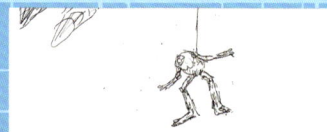

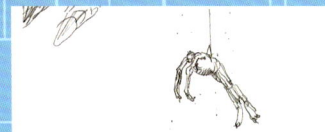

...THIS VERY DIFFICULT DOWN HERE.

MR. LINK SAYS, "CAN YOU STOP SWINGING SO MUCH?"

YES, WELL COULD YOU TELL MR. LINK I'M A LITTLE PREOCCUPIED AT THE MOMENT...

HE SAYS HE IS A LITTLE PREOCCUPIED AT THE MOMENT...

A MAJESTIC TEMPLE AND A FAST-CUT FINALE

Everyone who worked on the Himalayas section of the movie knew that the scenes involving the yeti temple and the ice bridge were going to involve months of meticulous planning and precise craftsmanship.

VFX supervisor Steve Emerson points out that building an impressive digital asset, such as the crumbling bridge seen in the movie, requires a great real-world maquette. "We are all stop-motion enthusiasts who believe in traditional filmmaking, so we wanted to get as much of the stuff in camera as we could. We want to do it in a way that honors this incredible art form."

So the team focused on building a smaller-scale temple for all the shot work, as well as portions of the bridge and gateway. They also built a full maquette of the ice bowl and scanned it to create a digital version.

"One of our biggest challenges was that everything is primarily white," says Emerson. "You only have a limited range before things clip out and you start losing detail on surfaces. We needed to bring out the patterning that the director wanted, but we had to figure out how much we could bring to the snow surface without losing realism. There was also the shadows being cast in the topology of that environment, not to mention the lighting of the temple."

FIG. 1

FIG. 2

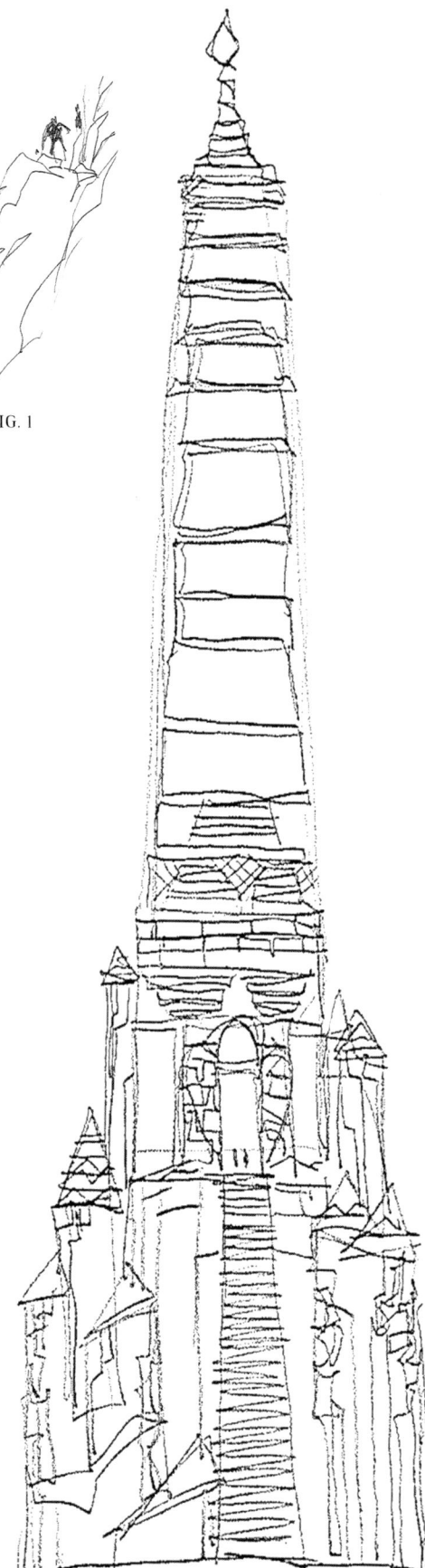

FIG. 3

PREVIOUS PAGES: Ross Stewart

FIGS. 1, 2 & 3: Santiago Montiel

OPPOSITE PAGE: Warwick Johnson Cadwell

FIG. 1

FIG. 2

FIG. 3

FIG. 4

FIG. 5

"I wanted to emulate some stylistic aspects of the ancient tapestries from the Himalayan region, while infusing them with the style of the film. I reimagined the yeti characters through the lens of a ceremonial fabric, and I wanted the characters to appear large in scale on the tapestry in order to emphasize the powerful and ominous reveal of the yetis in their mighty kingdom."

— MORGAN SCHWEITZER
GRAPHIC DESIGNER

FIG. 6

FIG. 7

FIG. 1: Juliaon Roels   FIGS. 2 & 3: Morgan Schweitzer   FIGS. 4 & 5: Kieron Thomas   FIG. 6: August Hall   FIG. 7: Santiago Montiel

ANIMATING ACTION

For animation supervisor Brad Schiff, the edge-of-your-seat sequence in which our heroes are suspended from a crumbling ice bridge proved to be quite a monumental undertaking. Animating an action scene is inherently difficult enough, but here the animators had to really focus on just how Link would hold on to a giant icicle for dear life.

"Every character is an embodiment of the animator who is animating it," Schiff explains. "We shot tons of reference footage to get into the right headspace. What we try to do is tap into the animator's artistic talent as an actor and bring it through these puppets. But then you have to add to that the technical challenge of figuring out how to put Link into this situation." To get the right kind of reference for the scene, Schiff and animators Kyle Rossi and Adam Fischer shot footage of themselves as they copied Link's interactions with the giant icicle. "We put the camera on a ladder and videotaped one another jumping and trying to hold on to a lamppost," says Schiff. Kyle Rossi actually wrapped his arms in tape so he could cling to—and climb—the lamppost. "That's the only way we were able to observe and capture all the subtle nuances of how the body would move and react in a situation like this," explains Schiff. "Our animators are actors who really have to perform through these puppets of silicone and steel."

Another clever solution for the sequence was using miniature three-inch-tall versions of the puppets. "Kingman Gallagher, RP [rapid proto-type] fabrication design lead, made minis that were spot-on replicas of Lionel, Adelina, and Link, and they had tiny armatures that gave us the same nuances," says Schiff. "We could comp them in for all the extreme wide shots, and you couldn't really tell that these weren't the larger puppets used in the other scenes. We had never done this before, and nobody would be the wiser."

Overall, Schiff says the whole sequence ended up exactly how he and his team hoped it would. "I think you really get a sense of the peril that these characters are facing," he says. "There was a lot of planning and ref-erencing involved, but all the different departments worked hard together so that you really believe that these characters are going through this very suspenseful situation as they hang from the sky bridge thousands of feet off the ground in the Himalayas."

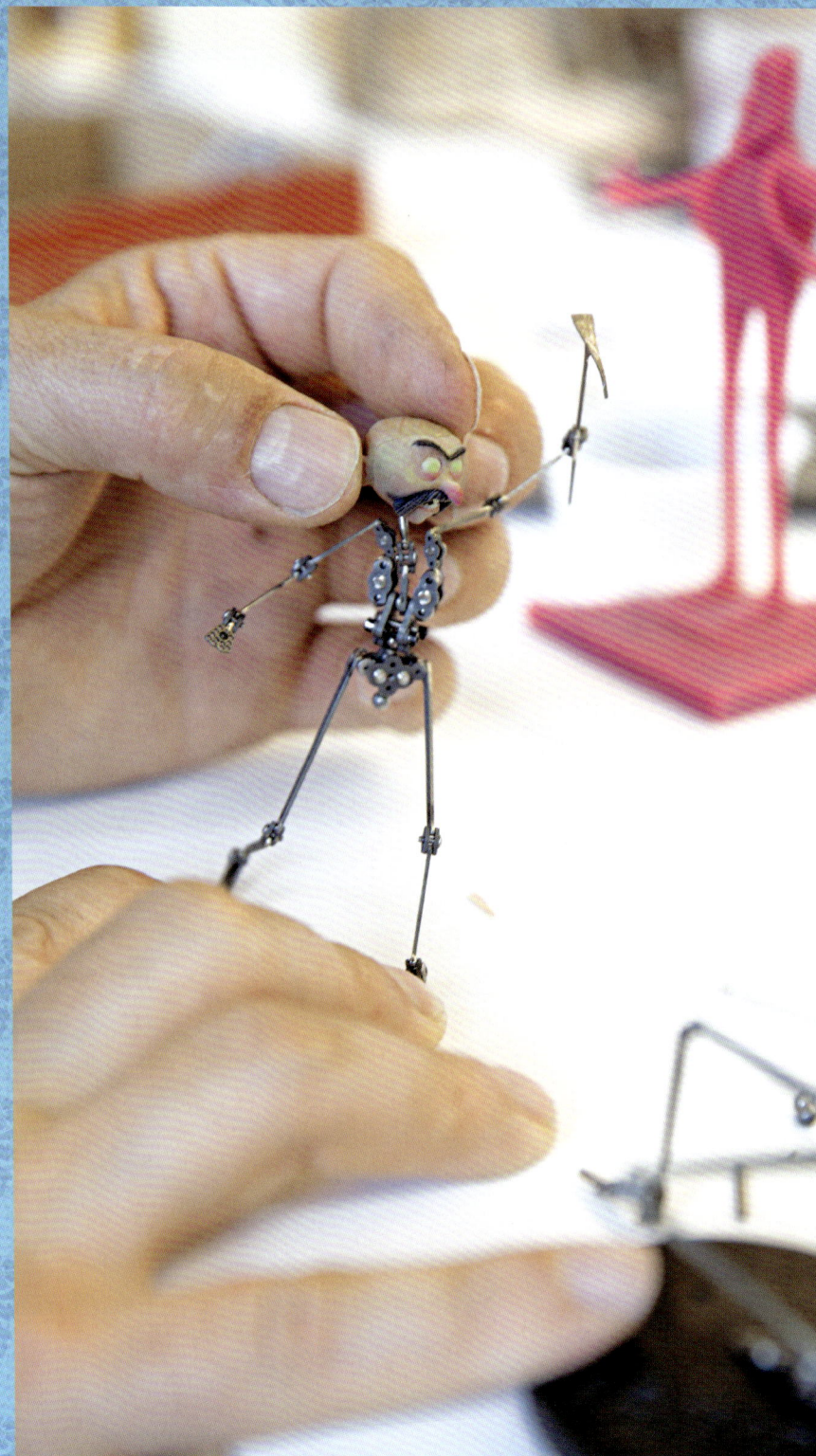

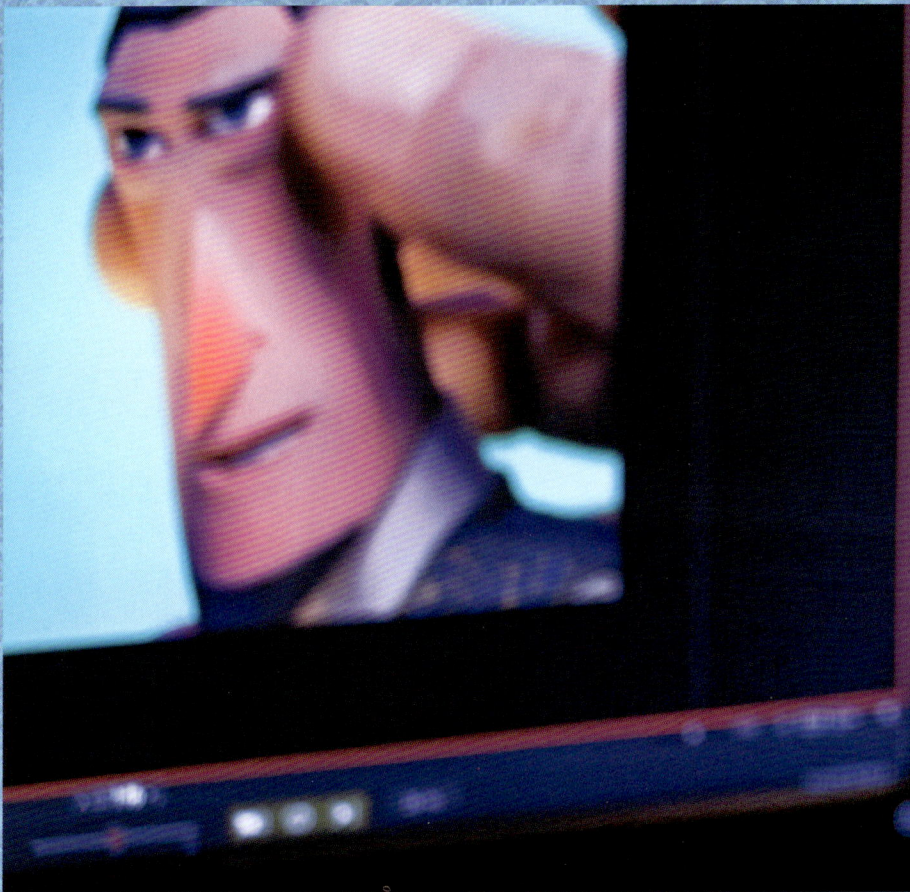

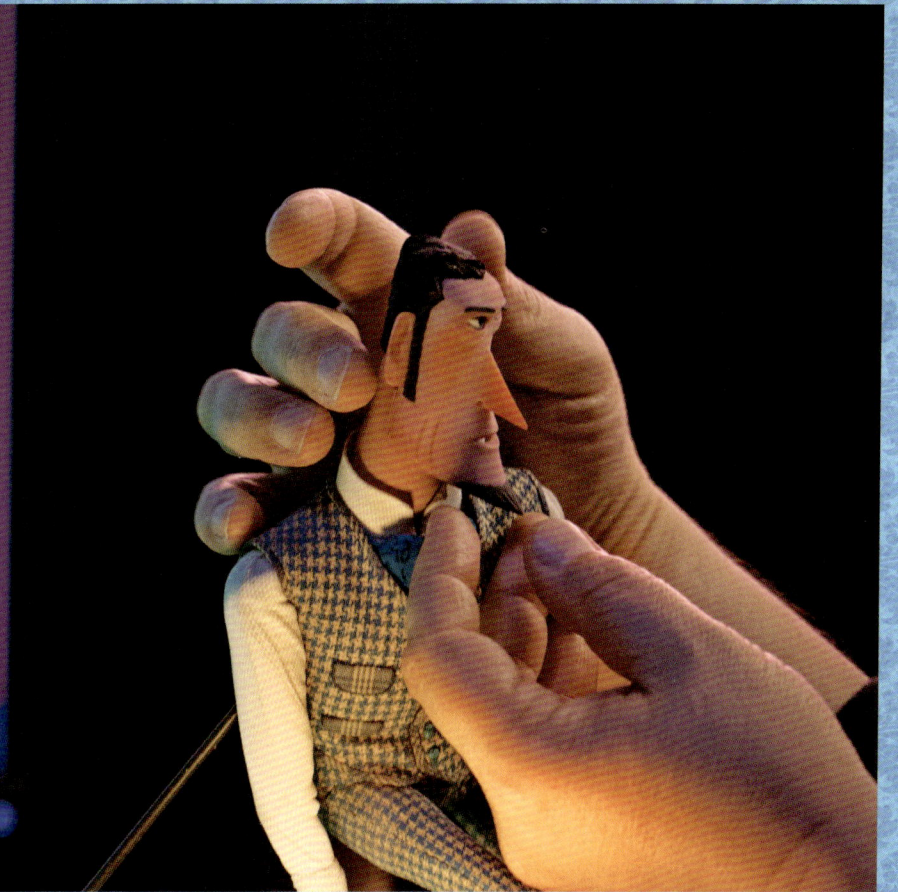

FIG. 1

INTRODUCING
GAMU

Providing the trio of adventurers the final key to their quest is a grumpy but charming elderly woman—with a chicken on her head. "She is the gatekeeper of the legend of Shangri-La," explains director Chris Butler. "In an early version of the script, her backstory was that her father had found the yetis. She watched him get taken away, and he never returned home again."

Butler says the character provides a bit of light relief before the climatic showdown so the audience can enjoy the main characters as a more unified group.

The character design was based on sketches by Butler, who was struck by a picture he'd seen of a wonderfully wizened old woman. "She had so many wrinkles, and her face looked like an engraving," he mentions. "So she became the starting point. You noticed these lines that were really quite graphic and so full of character." The sketches, in turn, inspired artist Trevor Dalmer to create paintings, which featured Gamu wearing colorful clothes based on traditional costumes of the region.

Even Gamu's home was designed carefully to reflect the way stones are stacked on top of one another in the far reaches of the Himalayas. "I did a lot of research on how these homes were built, and the architecture of these structures gave us another opportunity to incorporate our patterns in the backgrounds," says concept artist Santiago Montiel.

FIG. 1: Sandro Cleuzo

FIG. 2

FIG. 3

FIG. 2: Julian Nariño, Santiago Montiel, and Trevor Dalmer
FIG. 3: Jesse Gregg

FIG. 1

INTRODUCING
THE ELDER YETI

T he Elder (voiced by Emma Thompson) was designed to look enigmatic, intimidating, arrogant, and—since she is a distant relative of Link's—slightly goofy. The script paints a perfect picture of her: "She is as white and chilly as untouched snow. Hair flows around her like ceremonial robes, spilling down over the uppermost steps. Her expression is serene, but her eyes are shrewd and piercing."

Puppet sculptor Kent Melton explains, "I think she was the most challenging character to sculpt, because of her long, flowing hair. It took quite a lot of effort to figure out how to hold on to important things like her expressions and personality, while getting the right mechanics for flowing hair. Plus, it can't look too real, because she has to fit in with the world of this particular movie and stop-motion animation."

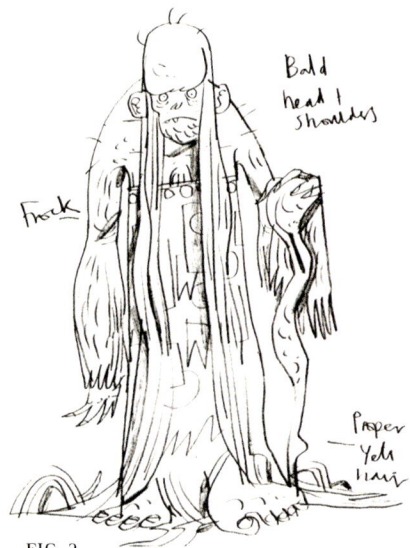

Bald head & shoulders

Frock

Proper Yeti hair.

FIG. 2

FIG. 3

FIG. 4

FIG. 5

FIG. 6

FIG. 1: Trevor Dalmer

FIGS. 2, 3 & 4: Warwick Johnson Cadwell

FIG. 5: Juliaon Roels

FIG. 6: Juliaon Roels and Chase Nichol

FOLLOWING PAGES: Santiago Montiel

THE YETI GUARDS

Since the yetis of Shangri-La are distant relatives of Link's, their design had to closely follow the Sasquatch's own. "My initial drawing of Link was described as a hairy avocado with legs," says director Chris Butler. "So, the yeti guards had to belong in the same family, but they had to be more serious, less cuddly, and ultimately, they end up being pretty cold and threatening. We took Link's design and made the guards more squarish shaped, more angular, with broad shoulders." The sharp angles on the yetis' nostrils and brow ridges helped hone their harsh demeanor.

Because the storyline demanded a small army of yetis who protect the Elder, the production team needed to come up with a way to re-create the crowd digitally. Overall, only three actual yetis were made—two were armored and one was naked. "We created two armored guards, and three faces for them," recalls Butler. "They all had to fit the same crowd scene, and the faces needed to be interchanged on the same body. We created three subtle changes in color—one was purple, the other bluer, and the third greenish—to create that whole army of yetis."

Butler showed his initial scribbles to Warwick Johnson Cadwell and Juliaon Roels, who drew up a veritable army of armored ape-men. These beautifully detailed line drawings provided a foundation upon which costume designer Deborah Cook could build. She created an intricate, almost ornamental armor for the characters, borrowing influences from a wide variety of sources. The black of their armor was also key; in their distaste for strangers, the yetis mirror the relationship between Sir Lionel and the Optimates Club. Butler sought to highlight this in their design. "Just like the lords are realized in black and white, with white hair and black tuxedos, the yetis are white with black armor," he points out. "I wanted our yetis to be equally unwelcoming to outsiders."

FIG. 2

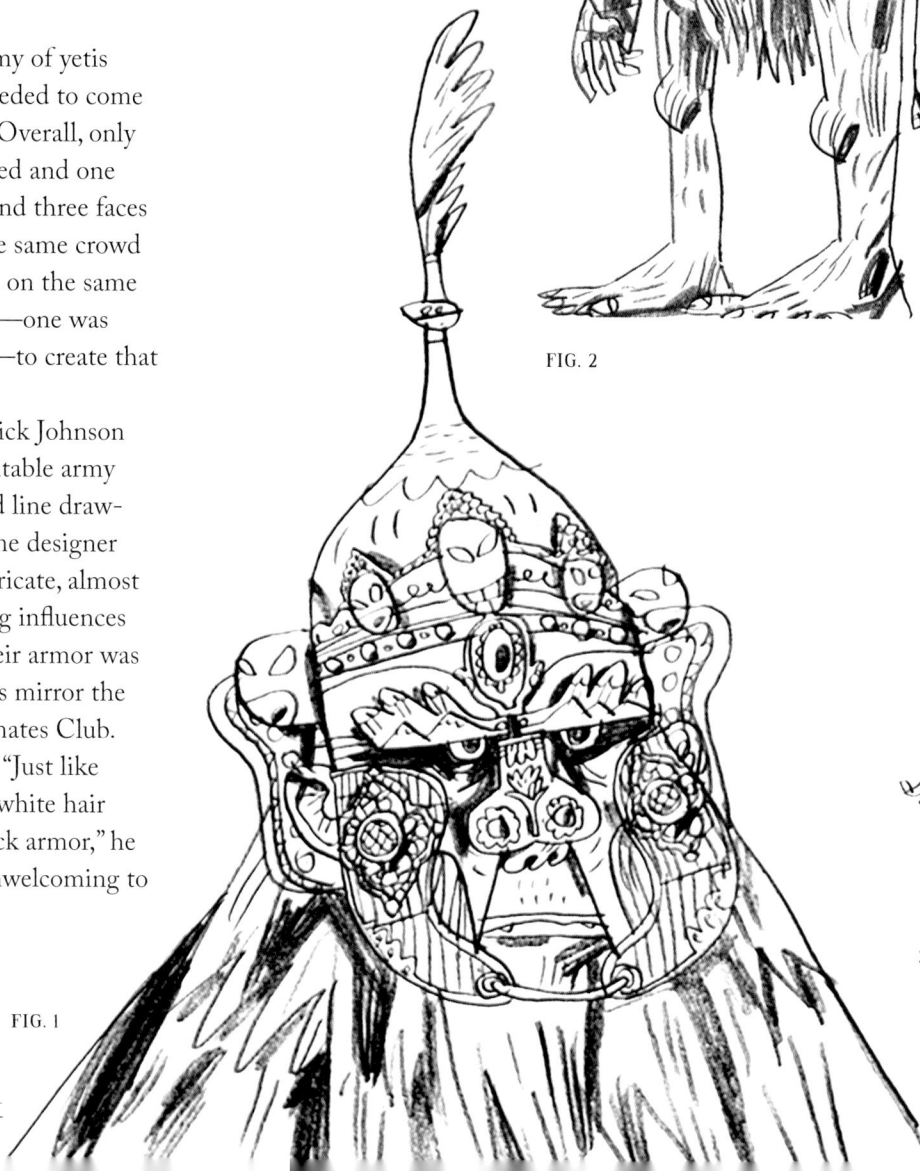

FIG. 1

FIG. 3

FIG. 4

"The idea was to use the graphic codes of Mr. Link and find what unites and opposes them. They are ancestral relatives and sacred creatures, impressive and imposing, and you needed to feel that in their design. We used ornaments and patterns to support this idea."

—— JULIAON ROELS
CHARACTER DESIGN AND CONCEPT ARTIST

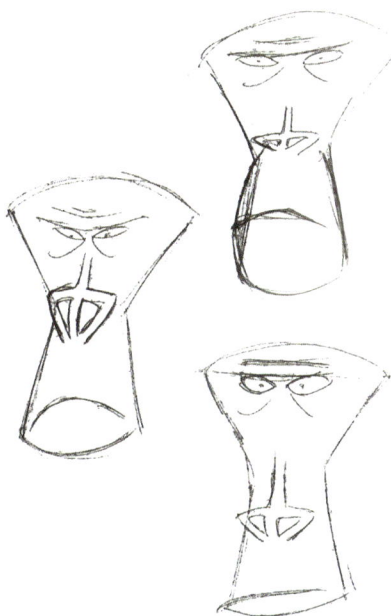

FIGS. 1, 2 & 3: Warwick Johnson Cadwell
FIG. 4: Juliaon Roels
FIG. 5: Chris Butler
FOLLOWING PAGES: Trevor Dalmer

FIG. 5

FIG. 2

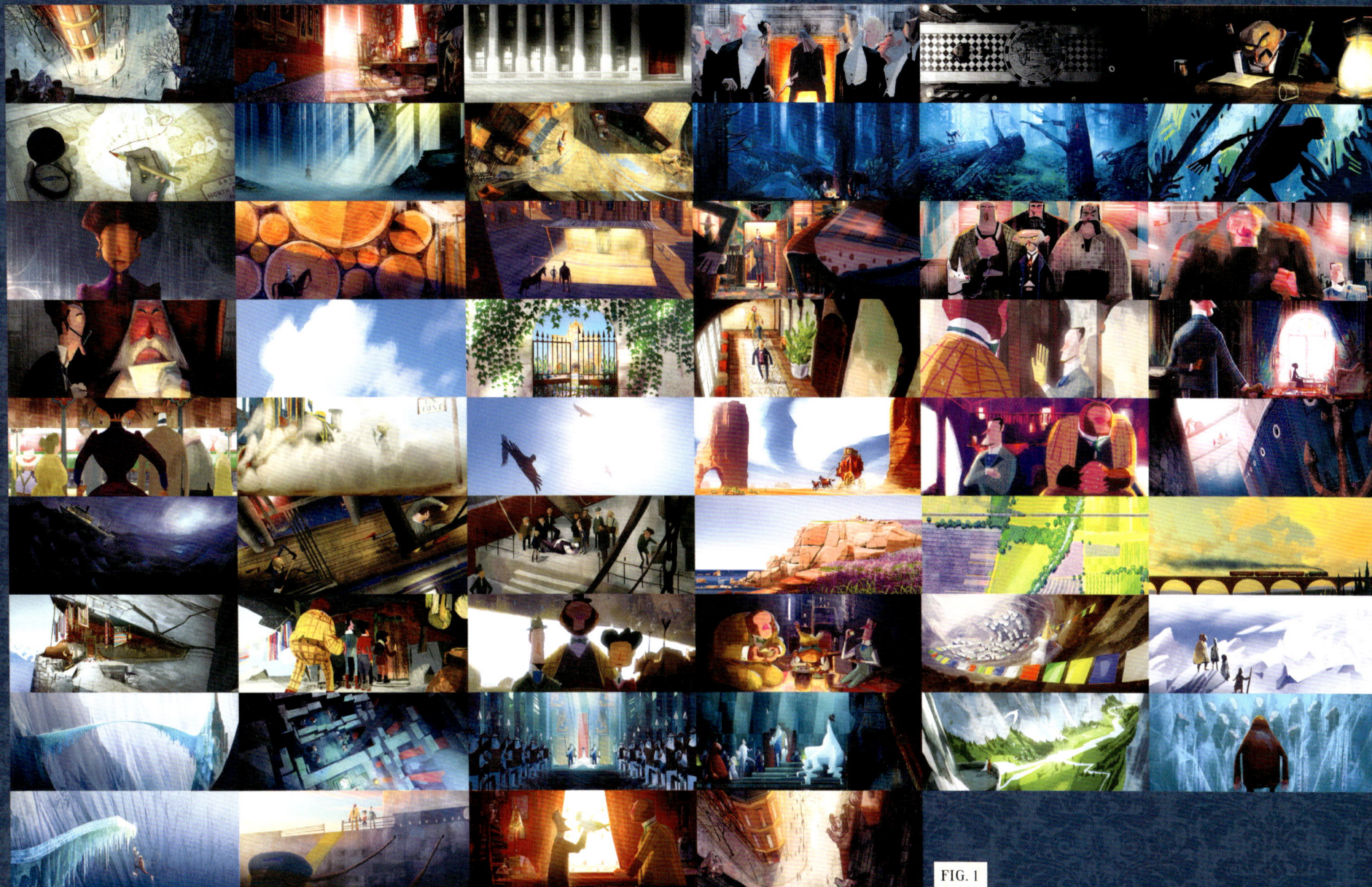

FIG. 1: Frames from the color script by David R. Bleich, Trevor Dalmer, and Nelson Lowry
FIG. 2: Hand-painted color studies by Nelson Lowry

Missing Link   Crew Photograph   2018

CONCLUSION

To call LAIKA's *Missing Link* a dazzling marriage between exquisite craftsmanship and bold, dauntless storytelling would be an understatement. Every frame of the studio's fifth stop-motion feature sparkles with creative ingenuity and artistry. As the film's writer-director, Chris Butler, mentions, he and his team wanted to venture into unchartered territories, pushing the boundaries of what stop-motion animation could do and what types of stories the medium could tell.

"When I started out, I wanted to make the definitive adventure movie in stop-motion," says Butler. "I wanted to step out of the shadows with this movie and create something striking and colorful that evoked the great classic nature photography of *National Geographic* magazine, along with the rollicking fun and audaciousness of Indiana Jones. The goal was to make a vivid, vibrant epic that was also a bit of a love letter to all the things that I loved as a kid."

Producer Arianne Sutner concludes, "Our crew worked incredibly hard on this film, finding ways to refine and improve upon our process and once again make something that's absolutely beautiful and unexpected. But it's the story of *Missing Link,* the universal themes, that really make me most proud. The notion of a big, beautiful world out there with a place in it for everyone. The need to recognize and celebrate our differences everywhere we go. This film explores these concepts so elegantly, and does it with true heart."

One thing's for sure: Once audiences feast their eyes on Lionel, Link, and Adelina's grand adventure, they'll be happy to follow them to the ends of the world—no matter which creatures they decide to visit next.

INSIGHT EDITIONS

PO Box 3088
San Rafael, CA 94912
www.insighteditions.com

Find us on Facebook: www.facebook.com/InsightEditions

Follow us on Twitter: @insighteditions

Published by Insight Editions, San Rafael, California, in 2019.

Library of Congress Cataloging-in-Publication Data available.

ISBN: 978-1-68383-809-8

Publisher: Raoul Goff
Associate Publisher: Vanessa Lopez
Creative Director: Chrissy Kwasnik
Junior Designer: Brooke McCullum
Project Editor: Greg Solano
Editorial Assistant: Jeric Llanes
Senior Production Editor: Elaine Ou
Senior Production Manager: Greg Steffen

Insight Editions would like to thank Chris Butler, Stephen Fry, Madeline Hampton, Martin Pelham, and Arianne Sutner.

ROOTS of PEACE   REPLANTED PAPER

Insight Editions, in association with Roots of Peace, will plant two trees for each tree used in the manufacturing of this book. Roots of Peace is an internationally renowned humanitarian organization dedicated to eradicating land mines worldwide and converting war-torn lands into productive farms and wildlife habitats. Roots of Peace will plant two million fruit and nut trees in Afghanistan and provide farmers there with the skills and support necessary for sustainable land use.

Manufactured in China by Insight Editions

10 9 8 7 6 5 4 3 2 1